An Unreasonable Notion of Desire

To Diane with my utmost admiration for your talent and integrity.

George Kaczender

An Unreasonable Notion of Desire

GEORGE KACZENDER

I would like to thank my editor,

   Rebecca Lowen,

For her talent and enthusiasm.

Library of Congress Number:		00-191248
ISBN #:	Hardcover	0-7388-2472-0
	Softcover	0-7388-2473-9

Cover drawing by George Kaczender

This book was printed in the United States of America.

To order additional copies of this book, contact:
Xlibris Corporation
1-888-7-XLIBRIS
www.Xlibris.com
Orders@Xlibris.com

To my wife, Joan

With love and admiration

"There is always some madness in love. But
there is also always some reason in madness."
NIETZSCHE, *Thus Spoke Zarathustra*

I.

ONCE OR TWICE a year, nature takes its revenge on Californians for destroying this land of paradise, physically and spiritually.

The Santa Ana winds have been blowing relentlessly for the past three days, day and night, drying out the air, the skin, the brains, heating up the city to nearly 100 degrees Fahrenheit. Young and old crowd the waiting rooms of allergy specialists, begging for relief. No one escapes.

I am incapable of doing any serious work or thinking under these conditions. My mind is becoming an alien entity unresponsive to my commands; it craves for an ideal environment.

I have been running my air-conditioner, humidifier and my air purifier non-stop in my high-rise condominium. But they don't prevent the insidious psychological effect of the winds. I feel demented.

The bathroom, with its high humidity, is the best place to be, though not without consequences. I can't stop gazing at my reflection in the bathroom mirror. The passage of time and its inevitable cruelty are clear as is the anxiety in my eyes. Could this be me? I feel healthy, bright and ageless as a child on his eleventh birthday. My mind rejects automatically the slightest evidence of physical deterioration. If I want to, I can behave and speak as a child, feel as a child; I can pretend to be eleven, sixteen or any age I want. But the mirror prevents me; the obvious signs of decay prevent me.

I hear the radio playing in my bedroom. The noise of the shower must have awakened Phoebe, or she is just too young and intelligent to sleep long hours. The channels change impatiently and then I hear Sade's melancholy voice.

The music doesn't distract me from my thoughts and worries. This morning, my reflection–my *unreal self*–destroys my illusions of youth, carves away my hopes, my dreams, in ruthless disregard for my struggling self.

In prehistoric times there must have been a moment when a tribesman discovered, for the first time, his reflection on the calm surface of a pond. What a moment that must have been! What if his face didn't compare favorably to those around him he considered physically striking, or to those he revered? Did he fly into an uncontrollable rage? Did he lose his mind and kill his family, his friends?

And what if he liked the reflected image? Perhaps it was a caveman and not a Greek poet who created the myth of Narcissus.

Phoebe turns up the volume to its limit, blasting Sade's seductive voice through the closed door, sending me an obvious message that I ignore–I am too busy torturing myself.

Without mirrors we are faceless, mere torsos with limbs. How can anyone develop without knowledge of his physiognomy? The self is carved into our faces. Whenever we study our reflection we reshape our egos; we discover ourselves. We may not like what we see but the reflection of our faces has a deep, accumulative effect on our mental development, on our lives.

I keep staring at my reflection. Because the mirror is slightly moist from the shower I appear to be covered with perspiration. My hair is almost gray. When did this happen?

I turn my head slightly, and notice small tufts of hair on my left ear. Phoebe, the young woman I date, frequently makes fun of these aberrations when I neglect to trim them. I must do everything I can to slow down the aging process, to camouflage time's ugly manifestations within the limits of good taste. I refuse to dye my hair. Vitamins, regular exercise and scissors are my only weapons. In Hollywood it is unforgivable for anybody to grow old, but one should age with dignity.

I open the bathroom door with the intention of greeting her but I choke on my words. She sits naked on the bed, relaxed and comfortable, cigarette in mouth, knees tucked under her perfectly conical breasts. Instead of saying *good morning* as I enter, she crosses her legs and blows smoke rings which hang seductively in the air. It is just a game. She enjoys mimicking *femme fatales* from old American *film noirs*.

Phoebe is in her early twenties but looks a little older, particularly when dressed. She studies cinema at USC under the guidance of an old friend of mine. We met when he invited me to visit his class and talk about my film-making experiences in Hollywood.

"You shouldn't have taken a shower yet," she admonishes, and, without taking her eyes off the towel wrapped around my waist, she extinguishes the cigarette. "I suffered one of those intense erotic dreams that linger on the rest of the day." She lazily stretches her arms toward the ceiling while yawning, reminding me of a cat thinking of attacking.

I approach the bed and stop at her feet. I am not in the mood to make love but the sight of her body excites me. The shape of her pubic hair, for one, is quite peculiar. It is the usual triangle on the pubis but her labia majora is devoid of hair for some freakish reason. But the most distinctive aspect of her appearance is the rare combination of blue eyes, black hair and chalk-white skin.

Despite all her remarkable qualities as a woman, Phoebe is not my girlfriend in the traditional sense of the word. We meet once in a while, see a movie, have dinner, and make love. Like most women of her age, she has her own circle of friends and boyfriends about whom I know nothing. Phoebe likes making love and she is ambitious. I don't have any illusions about her.

On her way out, rushing to a lecture, she gives me a perfunctory kiss in the doorway.

"Give me a call when you want to see the new Alan Renais film, and don't skip your exercise," she scolds me like a Jewish mother, then punches me in the stomach with such unexpected strength that I double up. "You need to lose a few pounds." She giggles at my ridiculous posture and runs to the elevator. I watch her youthful exuberance with envy.

I return to my apartment, turn the heat on underneath the kettle and grind some coffee. The day is already too hot to be drinking coffee but I know the strong scent will eliminate the residual odor of my night with Phoebe. Only when I am in love with a woman do I long for her smell. It is not that I am repulsed by Phoebe's odor; I could easily fall in love with her. But she is too young for me, and I must resist.

While waiting for the water to boil I take another shower disregarding completely California's unending water shortage.

After breakfast, I am anxious to get out of my flat. Despite the heat I decide to go for a walk and do some unnecessary shopping in Beverly Hills.

I live nearby in Century City, in an area that used to be the back lot of Twentieth Century Fox. When the studio system collapsed in the sixties, speculators bought up most of the studio's land and built expensive condominiums. It is a chic place to live if you can afford to buy. Ten years ago, when real estate in Los Angeles was still relatively affordable, I bought my place right after completing a big budget film in France.

Free of meetings and business lunch today, I decide to wander in Beverly Hills, one of the few areas in Los Angeles where you actually find people strolling and window-shopping. Being a European, I find the street life in California disappointing. My happiest moments in my childhood were spent roving the streets of Budapest, observing life in the city, watching people—mostly girls—in cafes, parks and everywhere, particularly in the old part of town.

My walk this morning will eventually take me to a book shop where I will browse, or perhaps buy some books on sale, or else find a first edition of the latest publication of a favorite writer. Between my film productions I spend tons of money on books; it is one of my innocent obsessions. They keep piling up in my study, some unread for a long time, some never read, others devoured immediately.

On the way out I check my mailbox. The normally peaceful lobby is already crowded with old widows in pink slippers and cotton, flower-patterned gowns, impatiently waiting for their junk mail. The postman, late this morning, is still sorting. I nod my head to some vaguely familiar faces and leave the building.

In the courtyard I pass a Mexican nurse pushing an invalid frozen in his wheel chair; he must be in his nineties. I see them every day when the wind is not too strong to spoil his day. He smiles. At first I think he recognizes me and this is his way of greeting, but as I pass him with a tentative nod of my head and a forced smile, his expression doesn't change; it must be a grimace of pain and suffering. I am wondering what keeps him going as I turn off to Olympic Boulevard, heading east.

She cannot be Marika, I am quite certain of that.

I remove my sunglasses to see her face better. Today I wear my extra-dense, custom-made shades to protect my eyes from the intense sunlight. Smog and pollution normally soften the light in Los Angeles, but today the Santa Ana winds have cleared the air and hardened the shadows.

She stands impatiently under the traffic light waiting for the change of colors. I am straight across from her at the corner of Wilshire and Canon Drive, wondering if I have gone insane. Marika, if she is still alive, would be a grand-mother. The woman under the traffic lights cannot be older than thirty-five. The hot wind must be roasting my brain; or am I having an anxiety attack?

The last time I saw Marika–for a fleeting moment–was the day I left Budapest, a few days after the Red Army had crushed the historic uprising in 1956. I have thought of her at least once every day since then. She was in her late twenties then, but if she were in her mid-thirties today, she would look exactly like that woman across the street at whom I am staring, nearly blinded, without my sunglasses. I am conscious of my pumping heart. Of course, she is not Marika. How could she be? The Tatar cheekbones, the straight blonde hair and large blue eyes are unmistakable, but most of the women in Beverly Hills look like her. No, it is not the bone structure or the hair color that have made me think of Marika; there is much more to this woman. It is the slightly sardonic curve of the mouth, the shape of the lips and their pneumatic promise, the eyes that seem ceaselessly surprised. The total effect of all the parts makes the resemblance astonishing.

The wait for the lights to change is interminable. A small crowd gathers around me and also around the woman across the street, partially blocking my view. When my concentration on her face momentarily breaks, I become conscious of my nausea. As I search for an explanation, I notice that the woman standing next to me exudes an amalgam of cheap, sweet perfume and decomposed perspiration. I scrutinize her from the corner of my eyes. She is heavily made up: lips too red, powdered face too white. She must be in her late fifties. A large floppy hat shadows a face mutilated by numerous cosmetic surgeons. A failed movie star made repulsive by excessive narcissism and old age? I quickly turn away.

A shove from bystanders redirects my gaze to the traffic light. It has turned green. I focus my attention again on the woman who looks like Marika; she has just stepped off the curb and is coming toward me. In a few seconds I will be facing her in the middle of the street. I forget my nausea as my heartbeat accelerates.

A gentleman with good upbringing does not accost a strange woman on Wilshire Boulevard at ten in the morning. The thought of doing so shouldn't even cross my mind. In Budapest you might consider it if it is a Sunday morning on the Danube Corso where people used to stroll to show off their fashionable attire and, perhaps, meet the dreams of their lives. But not in America.

As if weightless, I feel myself being carried by the crowd. Am I going to faint? How absurd. My mind cannot control the adrenaline surge, the potentially lethal biochemistry of the glands. I have learned to control a toothache or a head cold but not the adrenal medulla.

Despite my direct gaze, the woman doesn't even throw me a quick glance as I pass by. I look back over my shoulder hoping that my need to be acknowledged will impel her to turn around, but she continues walking.

I should stop trying to convince myself that I can transmit thoughts. Telepathy only works when the content of the transmission is unimportant, when say, you tell your wife of fifteen years, "Let's see a movie tonight!" and she instantly responds, "Was just going to suggest that; isn't that amazing?" No, not at all. I read books on parapsychology when I was young and it was fashionable. Then, I believed it to be a science. Little did I know. The results of the experiments at some universities were inconsistent and unrepeatable. They didn't live up to the rigors of empirical scrutiny.

Slowly, the studies were abandoned and for the past ten years I haven't heard or seen a word on the subject.

There is pride and purpose in her walk. I attempt a smile, but my facial muscles don't respond to the command exerted by my brain cells; the Santa Ana winds have incapacitated them.

Who is she? All that self-confidence in her stride irritates me, disturbs me, too.

Was she born with so much self-confidence or did she acquire it imperceptibly through education? A heated argument these days among scientists that gets us nowhere. She must be the offspring of wealthy, Protestant parents with lineage back to the Boston Tea Party. She couldn't have been brought up in California; it is not in her walk—not a trace of tartness or provocation.

I stand at the corner helplessly watching her walk out of my life again. Again? Why again? I don't even know her. It has taken me a lifetime to build up my self-confidence and reduce my neuroses to a level I can cope with on a daily basis. I still experience serious relapses, particularly when I don't work. Or, I should say, when I am out of work, when I don't get paid for my work. I always work on something related to film-making: I write screenplays that don't often sell, research films that rarely get produced, develop ideas with writers that never become screenplays. My work ethic doesn't permit me to read a book, or have fun, or live my life without applying the experience to film making. I don't enjoy life enough for its own sake. This is known as "the creative mentality". Does it really apply to me? It may be just guilt. But what is the root of this guilt?

I was born in the year Adolf Hitler came to power—perfect timing for a Jew. My mother was already pregnant with me when the Nazis burned down the Reichstag. I often wondered, had she realized what was to follow, would she have aborted me? I never asked her the question. My parents lacked the foresight, or more accurately the outlandish imagination, to predict the Holocaust. Not even the sages of the day dared to think human beings might be equipped with the capacity for such evil.

It was a Wednesday. Not a particularly exciting day of the week to be born. I wish it had been a Friday, or a Saturday; perhaps my life would have taken an entirely different course. Wednesday being the fourth day of the week, the pleasures of the weekend are already forgotten, and yet the end of the week is still remote. This makes Wednesday a day of drudgery, unrelieved by expectation or pleasant memory. It is an embarrassing birthday for a creative person. Still, perhaps Wednesday has some positive mythical significance. The Kabbala, I am certain, must have the answer.

In my twenties, whenever I was depressed, I picked up a book on psychology or on the occult. I started fantasizing about miracles that would drastically change my bad fortune, solve all my problems overnight. It was a childish way of thinking but I had heard and read about people who experienced unusual turns of events in their lives brought on by some extraordinary coincidence. Encountering that woman, who resembles Marika so much, is an obvious coincidence. But is it really? If I didn't think about Marika every day I wouldn't have paid attention to the woman when she passed by me. Was it predestination, or my will to meet someone like her that had brought on the encounter a minute ago?

Before I lose sight of her I have to make a quick decision. But I immediately realize that it is already made for me. In my mind's eye I see her face that mirrors forty years of fantasy and pain—the pain of her absence from my life. If I do not consume this pain, my fantasies will surely take over and destroy whatever is left of my rational mind. This opportunity will not repeat itself; it is a divine gesture I must take seriously lest the revenge of the furies be wreaked on my reason.

Just before the light changes to red I step back off the curb and follow her. The distance is safe enough to conceal my intentions though I don't yet know exactly what they are.

Now that I have made a decision I feel much better physically. My legs are steady, the nausea is gone and my heartbeat is normal. My mind still races, though, and fights images from unfulfilled fantasies distorted by a tormenting reality.

The winds continue to blow heat. I feel as if I am pushing against a wall of sunlight: the photons seem to have solidified against my body. They are no longer waves or particles but an impenetrable barrier. I put on my sunglasses to ease the pain in my retina.

As I walk behind her, I believe my confidence is not going to fail me this time; in fact, I find it rather easy to maintain without any trauma to my sensibilities. I have traveled a long road in my confidence-building—a lifelong education to counter the effects of early childhood experiences.

My first important memories go back to age three. I remember my parents and relatives discussing the persecution of Jews in Europe and ways to prepare ourselves for survival of a Nazi occupation of Hungary. They even talked about immigrating to Australia. The necessity of fleeing to stay alive was thus implanted in my mind and has stayed with me all my life.

Our Hungarian identity was taken for granted in our family, but being Jewish became the focus of our lives. It took me a few more years to understand the difference. History, the way I experienced it, didn't help build self-confidence.

It is quite easy to follow her. The white, tailored suit reflects so much light that her distant image appears ghost-like. She radiates enormous energy. I simply lock into her magnetic field and get pulled along, ignoring the traffic, the European luxury cars, the pink and white buildings mixed with glass tubes that penetrate threateningly the blue space. Offices for the dream makers.

The right-wing social critics say that film people are dangerous, that society needs to censor and regulate their production of fantasies. Having lived under Fascism and Communism, I very much disagree. Society must not censor; the artist himself has to make ethical choices. It is more important to reach for truth than to be concerned about its effect on the innocent or the evil-minded. After all, interpretation of art is a highly individual act, a creative process itself, just as is misinterpretation. Concealment of truth is unethical for an artist. Of this Hollywood has always been guilty, and for a long time I was too.

I see her entering a medical building. She must be rushing for an appointment with her gynecologist—a routine check-up. Or perhaps she is pregnant. It does not cross my mind that she may be happily married. Why wouldn't she be married? She is beautiful and intelligent. Yes, I can tell. It is all in her eyes, her gait. She carries the spark.

Perhaps she is dying of some horrible disease? But why do I think of death when I should be rejoicing? I have just found Marika's double. I've been looking for this person for decades. She is going to have her teeth cleaned, those perfect pearls in her mouth—that's it.

I hurry toward the entrance and push through the revolving door. A weasel-like salesman on his way out nearly gets squeezed between one of the slats and the door. His box of samples prevents his arm from being crushed. He threatens me with his fist from the sidewalk but I pretend not to noticed.

For a few moments I am disoriented in the dark lobby. Then I see the white penumbra slip through the closing elevator doors, escaping from my sight. This quest cannot end here. I rush to the large, unattractive uniformed guard seated behind the marble information desk like an ugly Buddha amidst a welter of TV monitors and telephones. I ask him about the beautiful blonde woman in the white suit who just slipped into the elevator. It's my last chance.

"Dr. Atwill," he says flatly, but I can detect in his eyes the lewd images he contemplates. Am I already jealous? Not of this grotesque creature—what's the matter with me?

"Where is her office?" I ask brusquely.

"Seventeenth floor," he mutters and turns back to "*The Price is Right*" on a nine-inch black and white TV set. I stay motionless for a moment while I digest the information. What kind of a doctor is she? Never mind! A stroke of good fortune—she won't slip away from me for sure. I lean against the marble desk top, let my palms absorb the coldness of the stone and restore my blood temperature to normal.

"Thank you," I say quietly, but I don't move. I feel much better. I must make a decision quickly otherwise the uniform will become suspicious of my passive behavior and will ring for more uniforms. They act fast when it comes to crazies in Beverly Hills. I don't consider myself crazy but my behavior at this moment could be construed as out of line.

I'm not a hypochondriac but elevators in medical buildings always worry me. I assume most people in them are sick and that the enclosed airspace is contaminated with their breath. Nonetheless, I step into a full one and take in the sight. There is the obligatory octogenarian widow, shrunk by severe osteoporosis to the size and shape of a Disney witch and made up like a marionette. She smiles at me, asking for forgiveness. Is this what I am going to become? Then there is a mother, at least three hundred pounds, wearing pea-green jersey pants and a sweatshirt without a bra, holding her wailing six year old and perspiring profusely. She tries to conceal her embarrassment by ignoring the brat. A pretty nurse with a stethoscope dangling from her neck stands at the control panel, projecting a sense of importance. A young, blue-collar worker behind her stares at her pert ass and holds his bandaged thumb up in the air as if to demonstrate to all in the elevator the condition and martyrdom of the working class. It is a long trip up to the seventeenth; the elevator stops at nearly every floor. Doctors and nurses step in and out, patients come and go carrying large X-ray results with a mixture of pride and fear. Two men in their sixties discuss their operations, each vying for the greater sense of heroic survival against the odds.

It becomes difficult to breathe as the elevator ascends. It seems that I will never get there. Perhaps this elevator doesn't go to the seventeenth floor. My mind slips into a wakeful nightmare.

Then just before carbon dioxide saturates the box, I reach my destination. Slightly dizzy—the first sign of asphyxiation—I step out in the company of anxious patients who, knowing where they are going, scatter in both directions. It hits me suddenly that I forgot to ask Buddha her office number. I stand in front of the closed doors of the elevator shaft like an idiot, trying to decide which way to go. The Directory on the wall across from the elevator doesn't list the names of the physicians. Waiting for the elevator with his mother, a boy of about ten years old with large, black-rimmed glasses, keeps staring at me. I must have given him the impression that I am lost. His bespectacled mother gives him a tug and he averts his eyes.

I decide to go to the right. When in doubt, rely on the intrinsic meaning of the word. It turns out to be the wrong way. The corridors are long and go in a circle. In ten minutes I end up where I started out on this embarrassing journey. I stopped at every door to check the name plates. They read exactly like the names on law office doors, with half a dozen doctors occupying each office. I never realized it before, but doctors operate on the same corporate principle as attorneys.

Her name is on a door by itself. The first good sign. Dr. Cass Atwill is a psychiatrist. I chuckle at the irony and can't help thinking that I have come to the right place. I can still change my mind, turn my back on the irresistible impulse which brought me here. I'll be able to control it, I tell myself. But do I want to? I may never again chance such an opportunity.

I enter. It's not what I expect to see in a doctor's waiting room situated in a modern medical building. I have stepped into another world, mysterious and forbidding.

Well-chosen, comfortable-looking antiques fill the room. The royal blue and burgundy velvet upholstery matches the Persian rugs that cover the dark parquet floor. Original paintings fill the wall space and sculptures of various sizes sit on tables and on floor stands. What is most remarkable about the paintings is not their authenticity and obvious value but their intent. They all depict, or attempt to penetrate, the viewer's subconscious. Of course, all good art aspires to this, but these works have clearly been chosen to do just this. Alone in the room, I fall immediately under their spell.

Soon I become conscious of the agonizingly dense silence. Still at the entrance, rooted to the floor, I try to orient myself. The low-key lights soothe my nerves. I am surprised how calm and rational I have suddenly become.

A tall emaciated woman comes through one of the many doors. Her gray hair is combed into a French bun which makes her already severe looks even more arresting. How did she know I entered the waiting room? The office is equipped with hidden electronic devices, I am guessing.

"You must have lost your way, sir," she says with a soft alto voice that reverberates through my entire body. For a moment I am speechless, then I remind myself that I am a film director who is supposed to be in control of complex situations.

"I believe I am in the right place," I say in a firm voice. Over the years I have learned to disguise trepidation in my voice and gestures. Working as a director in a second language, even after thirty years, creates certain anxieties, but in the past five years I have improved considerably. Perhaps life in Los Angeles is therapeutic. "I'd like to set up an appointment with Doctor Atwill."

"Well," she says, staring at my tennis shoes with obvious displeasure, "do you have a referral from your physician?"

"I don't have one, I'm afraid. I've never been sick." She cocks her head slightly, and dilates her nostrils as if she just noticed particles of intestinal gas floating in the air.

"Dr. Atwill requires, without exception, that her patients be referred by physicians."

"Thank you," I say, and leave.

It's eight o'clock in the evening. I haven't eaten dinner yet. My morning experience with Dr. Atwill and her secretary ruined my appetite and reduced me to a near catatonic state. I've been glued to a chair in my study since I left her office, trying to work out a safe and reasonable strategy to approach her without making a complete fool of myself. I struggled for most of the afternoon to wipe her image out of my mind but it didn't work; her face is so perfectly blended with Marika's that the two have become one maddening woman, like two pictures superimposed in a faultless match. I can't separate them.

Is my preoccupation with Dr. Atwill self-generated, or is it out of my control? Perhaps both. I feel driven into a dangerous fixation. Over the years I have reconciled myself to the fact that Marika isn't part of my life anymore. Up to now, I have learned to live with her image innocently popping in and out of my mind from time to time. But now this woman throws me off balance, poisons my occasional daydreams replayed from the past with implausible prospects, injecting hopes of new experiences that shouldn't happen. Living with the memory of Marika has been my worst punishment. Do I now search for something beyond the fulfillment of these nagging fantasies?

I tried to read and work this afternoon but I kept seeing Dr. Atwill's face as if it were being projected onto the screen of my brain. I am paralyzed. I shouldn't be alone. I could call Phoebe or a friend to keep me company. But in a way I enjoy my mental torture. My sexual fantasies are already shaped around Dr. Atwill and I feel I'd be betraying her if I called another woman to make love. But as much as I enjoy my suffering I must be practical and put an end to it. Also, I am hungry and don't want to dine by myself. Phoebe is an extrovert, a natural entertainer; I can just sit in silence across the table from her as she chatters about her studies, writing, and her experiences with her punk boyfriend.

I decide to call one of my friends, a physician, to set up an appointment for me this afternoon with Dr. Atwill. I was so restless all morning that I lost a tennis match to a friend who's never beat me. He's a producer with whom I've had a project for years but nothing has yet come of it. The subject is not right for Hollywood, we concluded.

* * *

II.

WINTERS IN HUNGARY were mostly temperate, unlike the winters I later experienced in Montreal. Often, we got through the entire season without snow or severe cold.

Thank God, the winter of 1945 was exceptionally cold in Budapest. It saved our lives.

I spent the last three months of the war hiding with my parents from the Nazis and the Hungarian Fascists, the Arrowcross, in a damp, filthy air-raid shelter. We had no food, no facilities to maintain decent hygiene. There was only fear of impending disaster, fear of our real identities being discovered, fear of hits by the Russian artilleries. And boredom for a child of ten locked up with strangers who smelled bad and looked depressed, all of them adults. I spent my days drawing airplanes in a small pocket book I carried with me everywhere.

In December 1944, the Red Army had surrounded the city and started blasting it day and night. Instead of retreating to the west, the Germans dug in, blew up all the bridges across the Danube and fought till the last German soldier perished in the street fights. They forced the Russians virtually to level the city. It was typical of Nazi fanaticism to sacrifice a beautiful city at a time when the outcome of the war was already inevitable.

Before the three of us went into hiding my father had escaped from a Hungarian forced labor camp that the Fascist government had set up before the Germans occupied Hungary. They didn't trust Jews to fight the war; instead, they worked them to death in mines and on road construction jobs where conditions were barbaric.

With the help of his friends, my father bought forged documents bearing typical gentile names and came back to the Budapest ghetto to fetch my mother and me. I hardly recognized him when he showed up one day sporting a large, peasant mustache. A significant number of middle-aged farmers weren't drafted into the army, not even in the final years, because they were needed to provide food for the fighting forces and the cities. With his blonde hair my father felt relatively safe on the streets.

His arrival was a godsend. Months before our reunion, the Germans and the Arrowcross had begun lining up the Jews in the ghetto to select them at random for deportation. They came to our apartment building a few times and called everyone downstairs into the courtyard. I knew from past experience that the soldiers didn't always come upstairs to search the apartments, either out of sheer laziness or because they assumed people would be afraid of instant retaliation were they found in their apartments. So when they came that September I decided not to go down with my mother.

This was the moment when I first began questioning the nature of reality. I sank deeper and deeper into a world of fantasy where I felt safe, where I nurtured an absolute conviction of survival. This conviction, encouraged by an imaginary guardian angel—omnipotent and ubiquitous—was so strong, so all-consuming that I withdrew altogether from normal activities with children and adults in fear of breaking the spell.

Miraculously, the soldiers let my mother go. She flashed a piece of paper at them stating the outlandish subterfuge that we were under the protection of the Swedish government. It was a copy of a copy of a copy, barely legible, but for the young Wermacht soldier who didn't know about the Wallenberg passes, it looked official. Had the SS troops come, she would have been taken to Auschwitz.

I don't know how many more times my mother and I would have escaped those line-ups if my father hadn't come.

There was another reason we survived. Hungary—always on the wrong side throughout history—was Germany's ally during the war. Admiral Horthy, Regent of Hungary, imposed most of the laws that the Nazis had in Germany: banning Jews from higher education and from business ownership, and imposing forced labor on men eligible for military service. Although Horthy was an anti-Semite, he didn't force Jews into concentration camps, and he didn't build gas chambers. For this reason, Hungarian Jews were luckier than those in Poland and Czechoslovakia.

In 1944 Hitler discovered that Admiral Horthy had began negotiations with the Allies to declare Hungary a neutral nation. He called Horthy to Berlin on a ruse, and while he was there the Nazis occupied Hungary. The head of the Arrowcross party, Ferenc Szalasi, took over the governing of the country.

It was not until Szalasi came to power—in March 1944—that the systematic elimination of the Hungarian Jews started. Jews who lived in small cities and towns were easily rounded up and shipped to German concentration camps, most of my relatives among them. But Budapest, the capital city, was a different matter.

The war wasn't going well for Germany. Too busy fighting and camouflaging their defeats to attend fully to the liquidation of Hungarian Jews, the Nazis left most of the work to the incompetent and disorganized local Fascists. Stalin had begun his counterattack on the eastern front, pushing the Germans west across Hungary. How the Hungarian Fascists at that time could still believe in a Nazi victory is incomprehensible. The opportunities for legalized murder and pillage of the Jews must have blinded them to reality. But time ran out for them. The Jews in the ghetto who survived disease and the scarcity of food and who miraculously escaped deportation, numbered more than the unfortunate Polish and Czech Jewry. There simply wasn't time to kill all the Hungarian Jews.

I was the only child in the air-raid shelter. Among the adults, none of whom we knew, may even have been fascist sympathizers. Though my father was fair and had grown that large mustache, my mother and I looked unmistakably Jewish with our dark, curly hair. My parents didn't elaborate on the possible grave consequences of a slip-up, but I was aware acutely of the risks they had taken. Still, the odds were for us. Had we stayed in the ghetto, the chances for survival would have been much smaller.

Ironically, we found out after the liberation that most of the people in that shelter were either Jews hiding with forged papers like us, or communists. In fact, the couple who took care of us were also communists—the husband a famous artist. We stayed in their third floor apartment until the relentless bombing by the Allied forces made it too risky.

One day, around Christmas, the building next door was badly hit during an air attack. I became hysterical, sure I was about to die. I am certain my parents felt the same way though they didn't show it. The next day we all went down to the shelter where our hosts introduced us as their guests from out of town.

Our sleeping arrangement in the shelter didn't leave much room for rest. In a remote corner, placed between a damp, dirty wall and a wooden beam which functioned as a buffer, we slept on a small cot, all three of us. Without the beam my mother, who was on the outside, would have rolled onto the floor. We managed through the night by sleeping on our sides. I wish I could remember the dreams and nightmares of that period in my life; they have been erased or deposited into the deepest layers of my subconscious.

No continuous flow of action, just bleary fragments of images and impressions from that period remain with me. For an eleven year old the situation was utterly incomprehensible, yet instinctively I accepted our condition. It is not that I didn't know who the enemy was, or who should win the war, or that we were hiding in mortal fear, but that I couldn't understand the hatred that had brought all this about.

Ceaseless hunger, boredom and fear of death were my prevalent preoccupations. I can't recall actually eating anything, though we must have fed ourselves with something. I don't even remember going to the bathroom in those days. The washroom was either so disgusting that I have repressed the experience, or else we didn't have much use for it, having little to digest. I don't even remember how we washed up, if at all. We must have stunk.

One night we awoke to a symphony of artillery fire. It sounded as if all the heavy guns of the Red Army had suddenly exploded outside the city with such force that instant devastation seemed inevitable. All three of us sat up on our cot and listened. I was paralyzed with fear, but once I detected in the semi-darkness my father's smiling face, I relaxed. He listened for awhile, then in a calm voice, that contrasted with his usual tone of concealed fear, he said, "This sounds good to me," and went back to sleep.

The siege lasted three days. On the morning of the third day, as if by command, the fireworks stopped suddenly and a peculiar silence descended on the city, a stillness full of expectation and hope. A staccato sound of submachine gun fire followed for a few hours, then silence set in again. My father's face was beaming with excitement. He turned to us and whispered, "They'll be here any minute."

As if on cue, the door to the air-raid shelter suddenly flew open and a troop of Russian soldiers rushed inside, pointing their still smoking *balalaikas* at us. They were dirty, ugly and excited. Having seen pictures of US soldiers in newspapers and newsreels before moving into the ghetto, I would have preferred *them* as liberators. My instinct, like most children's, was sharp. I sensed that this wasn't the end of our troubles. After a thorough search for German soldiers, booze, watches and women, they picked out a girl in her early twenties, took her to a storage room next door and gang raped her. When the poor girl returned, still crying, she told us they'd only had her sew a few buttons on their jackets.

For us, the sight of those soldiers was a most extraordinary relief. We had been waiting for that moment for over five years and now suddenly they were here liberating us from the Nazis and saving us from starvation.

My mother and father, tears in their eyes, hugged the soldiers as if they were close relatives on a surprise visit from a distant land. Nobody spoke Russian in Hungary in those days, so my mother talked to them in Yiddish, hoping one of them might be Jewish.

Watching the events unfold from a distance I was overwhelmed with a new feeling, a sense of serenity if only for a short time. I had believed since that day in September that I could rely on my guardian angel; I had always hoped that I would survive the war and persecution. I was smiling—probably the first time in years. The struggle for survival, the constant hunger pangs, the omnipresent filth, finally had come to an end. We were free again. I felt as weightless as a glider soaring on warm currents. Soon, we were going to eat meals cooked by my mother; I'd be able to sleep in my own bed; the terrifying noise of the air-raid sirens wouldn't wake me up every night.

We stayed in the shelter a few more days until my father judged it safe enough to venture outside. We could still hear the distant sounds of heavy artillery blasts but the machine-gun and rifle fire had mostly ceased.

No one had any conception about the physical condition of the city. Our old apartment building could have been in ruins. It was situated close to one of the most important railway stations in Budapest, in the center of the city—a critical strategic spot. We expected the worst.

It was cold and overcast on the streets, and relatively quiet when we first stepped out of the dark crypt that had sheltered us for months and into daylight. Only the occasional explosion from west of the Danube broke the dreamy silence. The air was still dense with the stink of sulfur and smoke from burning buildings. There was no civilian traffic; only tanks and military trucks carrying Russian troops drove by on the main arteries of the city. Burned out German tanks and collapsed buildings blocked the intersections of narrow side streets, preventing the life in them from resuming. Ghostlike figures scurried along the sidewalks hurrying with dread and anticipation toward their destinations. It was like the set of an opera before the singers stepped on stage: magical, with tension-filled anticipation of the unknown. I loved it. I decided to celebrate that day as my second birthday. That's why even today I love the month of January.

As we walked feverishly, my parents, well-conditioned to expect sudden dangers on the streets, kept close to the walls of the buildings. As always, my mother lagged behind, slightly overweight, unfit for any type of physical exercise. My father kept an eye on her and occasionally took her arm to ease her stride. I walked, abandoned. My guardian angel had proved my immortality; I had nothing to fear anymore.

In the distance I saw a group of people huddling over something in the middle of the street. When we reached them, my father stopped us. A glint appeared in his eyes. A dead horse was sprawled on the snow-covered street, partly frozen. Before the war, in certain areas of the city, horses were still used for transporting beer, ice, and produce.

Men armed with butcher knives were busy carving large chunks out of the frozen cadaver, preserved from decay. They eagerly wrapped the meat in old newspapers and rushed away in obvious excitement over what would be their first meal since liberation. Without hesitation, my father reached for his Swiss pocketknife and joined the amateur butchers. We watched him in silence as he struggled with the small blade, then my mother said resignedly, "We must eat some meat. Thank God it's cold this winter." I didn't say a word. I was so happy that I forgot I was starving.

We couldn't wait to get back to our old home. When we left, my mother had offered the apartment to a gentile couple, truly decent people, and trusted them with all our possessions. The husband had worked for my father before the Fascists closed down his business. They promised to return everything to us intact if we survived the Holocaust.

Well, we had survived but we didn't know if our building had. It wasn't a long walk, less than a mile. As we approached our street I could sense my parents' anxiety growing, but I knew in my heart that we'd find the place undamaged. It wasn't my talent for clairvoyance; it was a deep conviction that life from now on would be painless and continue exactly as it had left off. I had been deprived of a chunk of my childhood; this is what I expected in recompense.

When we stopped at the corner of Garay and Nefelejts Streets, my parents faltered, fearful of looking into our street and discovering complete devastation. I've often wondered if they had a contingency plan. I couldn't wait any longer and dashed around the corner. The building was standing just as we had left it.

"It's there!" I shouted and ran back to them. We quickened our steps; even my mother made an extra effort to keep up with us. I saw a smile appear on my father's face that made me feel secure again. My mother was crying—in joy, I think.

The wall of our building was riddled with bullet holes and all the windows had been broken by the impact of bombs exploding nearby. That was the only visible damage. Some of the other buildings on our street were completely leveled. Unfortunate tenants, like beggars, were picking out their belongings from under the rubble, salvaging whatever was left undamaged, or still useful.

We didn't run into any of our old neighbors as we crossed the courtyard and approached the worn staircase. The feigned pleasure of their greetings would have destroyed our joy of return. Most of the tenants in the building were hard nosed anti-Semites and later, after we had settled in our apartment, my mother heard some gossip that some of our neighbors were displeased that we survived the Nazis.

Marika was thirteen years old when I first saw her. It was a momentous day, but not only because I caught her eyes for the first time as she watched us lug our few pathetic posessions back to our old apartment. She stood behind her family's unwashed kitchen window, gazing sadly out of the ground floor apartment into the courtyard, bored, hoping to see signs of life on that drab winter day. She must have sensed a beginning when our eyes met. She smiled at me, tentatively at first, then with the openness only children possess. They must be new tenants, I thought. A middle-aged lady with bleached hair had lived there before. She used to keep a bottle full of leeches in her window. I remember we often laughed at her eccentricities and her snobbish demeanor. In her youth she had been a vaudville actress. She must have died during the war or moved to the country. I wondered what happened to her white poodle.

* * *

III.

I AM SEARCHING MY closet for something original and seductive to wear but nothing looks right. Perhaps I should go out and buy a new suit at Armani. Ridiculous. I don't want to come off as an Italian gigolo or a Hollywood agent. On the other hand, I don't want to wear California casual either. I'd like to make a good, clean impression on her. Meeting a shrink the first time is a risky proposition. One is aware acutely that, in a split second, the psychiatrist will make a judgement based on appearance, looks, demeanor, posture, voice and the rest of it.

As I debate this vital issue with myself, Dr. Atwill's image flashes through my mind. I can see her coming toward me at the intersection of Wilshire and Canon, dressed in white. Yes, yes, how stupid of me; why didn't I think of it immediately? My white suit—she'll understand the symbolism. The one I bought in Paris and hardly wore in fear of appearing to copy Tom Wolfe.

I take my white Ungaro suit out of its dust cover and slip into the pants. Amazingly, they still fit me. A couple of cinema tickets surprise me as I put my hand into the right pocket of the jacket. The Avco theaters in Westwood. I can't recall the person I took along, nor the title of the movie. I search for more evidence in the pockets but find none. It'll come back to me soon, I keep reassuring myself but it doesn't. Suddenly I become anxious. Why is retrieving this memory so important to me? Am I testing my recall? Has my daily loss of brain cells increased lately? My God!

This time Dr. Atwill's secretary treats me with icy cordiality.

"The Doctor will be with you in a few minutes, Mr. Fodor," she says, and does a quick turn as if to catch someone fingering one of the artworks. I am left alone with my anxiety. It dawns on me that I am not well prepared for this interview. I haven't yet figured out what I'll say if she asks me how I came to know about her. I'll have to tell her the truth sooner or later—just not today.

Normally when I visit a dentist or a doctor I take a magazine or book along. I don't want to rely on the outdated news or banal fashion magazines for entertainment that you always find in the waiting rooms. I also worry about the germs. When I thumb through those well-worn issues of *Time* or *People* in the waiting room of an ear, nose and throat specialist, I can't help worry that the latest flu virus may be sticking to my fingers. All it takes is a careless touch to the eyes or nose and the virus is soon swimming in your bloodstream.

Since the nature of my visit to Dr. Atwill is other than medical, I've come without any reading material. I know it is not logical but I want to focus all my mental energy on the interview. Even if wanted to read a magazine—after all, manic depression and schizophrenia are not contagious at the moment—I couldn't. Odd. I wonder why she deprives her patients of printed matter? Must be to encourage them to be punctual. She wants them to respect time, the bitch goddess of science; she doesn't want her rich, showbiz neurotics to fritter it away thumbing through magazines in her waiting room. Treating them this way she doesn't need to feel guilty when she interrupts a session on the dot of the hour and throws her patient out before he's finished the interpretation of his latest dream. Shrinks are ruthless about time, as if being punctual were a part of their treatment, reinforcing in the patient's mind the idea that every second of one's life must be spent productively. Not that I've had any first-hand experience, but when I used to live in Montreal I knew a number of psychiatrists.

I check my watch: I am ten minutes early. No wonder Dr. Atwill's Cerberus was icy when I arrived. My eyes sweep the room and are arrested by a painting. It is a Balthus—but a wonderful fake. I know the original is in a European private collection. He is among my most cherished artists whose work deeply affects me, evokes buried images from my subconscious. I know a shop on Melrose Avenue that sells brilliantly executed forgeries of major artists to the middle class and to culture snobs. You must be an expert to be able to distinguish between an original Picasso and a fake one.

The painting depicts a young girl sitting on a chair in a sexually provocative pose. She leans against a large, comfortable cushion, her head held straight by the entwined palms of her hand. Her right foot rests on the floor while her left leg is pulled up on the chair causing her skirt to slip up to her waist and revealing the white panties. Her face is not particularly beautiful; in fact, it's rather plain. Her eyes are closed as if daydreaming, imagining sexual ecstasy. Next to the chair, a well-fed ginger cat slurps milk from a small plate, adding another strong, sexual metaphor to the image.

The subtext is obvious but also innocent; it depends, of course, on the viewer's own sexual proclivities.

Almost everything in the picture is somberly colored except her short, red skirt—a perfect frame for her pristine white panties. Her slippers are also red which helps the eyes focus on her crotch. I know this provocative and controversial painting very well. The title of the piece is *Therese Revant.*

I rise from the armchair and move closer to the painting even though I can see it well enough from where I am sitting.

From close range I begin to see details on the periphery of the composition. On the left side of the painting, next to the girl's chair, stand a table and another chair, both only half-visible. A red and beige container and two vases rest on the table. One vase is dark brown and of average size, and the other, made of glass, is tall and thin, a perfect phallic symbol. There is one object on the canvas that mystifies me. A crumpled towel, or cloth of some sort, hangs from the table and is about to fall on the floor. It looks dirty, or perhaps it's just the way the shadows are painted. I can't figure out what it represents. Also, there are no flowers in the vases. I imagine that the flower is hidden behind her white panties.

I think to myself that Balthus is a genius.

"Do you like the painting, Mr. Fodor?" I pivot as if jerked by a puppeteer to

z

face the voice behind me. It's Dr. Atwill, this time in a rusty-red suit, not unlike the color of the skirt on the girl in the painting. She is beautiful. A perfectly chiseled face with high cheekbones, eyes large and wide apart, an ideal nose and a moderately sensual mouth. Her hair is pulled back conservatively and her make-up is slight. She must be conscious of being too perfect and beautiful for a shrink. Her sheer presence could possibly do more harm to her patients than all their rotten childhood and adult experiences put together. I don't smell any perfume on her, thank God. She intentionally avoids all possible sexual provocations. Probably she encountered trouble in the past with her patients falling desperately in love with her. I think she is in the wrong business. She should be working for one of the major TV networks as a reporter, or as an anchor woman and married to a Hollywood star, like Maria Shriver, and living happily ever after. What is she doing here, trying to cure the damaged souls and psyches of Tinsel Town?

"Love Balthus," I say without thinking. My first *faux pas.* Now she knows more about me than I would have let on in a month of therapy. I've given nearly everything away at once. At this instant I realize why there isn't any reading material in the waiting room. She is clever. Preceding her sessions she prepares the patients' psyches with works of art that unsettle them enough so that they respond to her analytical methods. I am mad at myself for being so careless in the presence of a shrink. It must show on my face for she smiles as she extends her hand—warm and padded like a cat's paw. Her handshake is firm.

She leads me into her inner office. Large, red velvet curtains partially block the sunlight and help create a mystical atmosphere. A Persian rug covers the leather couch, as in Freud's famous consulting room; another covers the floor. The furniture is dark and antique, mostly baroque. Bookshelves cover the walls. African statuettes and small ancient sculptures are lined up along her cluttered desk, just as on Freud's desk, if I remember it correctly from his biography.

She settles comfortably in a big chair behind the desk and points to an armchair facing her.

"Have a seat. I hope that chair is comfortable enough."

"Thank you," I say, and sit in the chair that is, in fact, painfully uncomfortable, as are most antique chairs. "You look incongruous in this office," I add, and smile at her.

"This used to be my father's office. When he died a few years ago I took it over. I feel good here, it's conducive to contemplative work."

"For me the effect is contradictory. It calms me, and at the same time disturbs me." As soon as I say this I realize I've made another mistake. I notice her subtle reaction to my comment. To rectify my carelessness I come up with a lukewarm, if not outright silly line.

"One can't be careful enough when talking to a psychiatrist." I try to smile but she isn't polite enough to fake appreciation of my lame joke. She looks at me with the neutral expression that only shrinks can muster.

"What do you find disturbing about this office?" She asks, a hint of challenge in her voice.

"The artwork has been carefully selected to stir up the subconscious," I reply with as much self-confidence as I can mobilize under stress.

"But that's exactly my job: to bring the content of my patients' subconscious to the surface," she says with a gentle but wicked smile. I decide to stay silent. I am not going to fall deeper into her net. The less I say the better. It is her job to trap the patients; she's been practicing it for God knows how long.

"Let's not get off on too many tangents," announces the Doctor after a long pause, with a slight edge to her voice. The smile has disappeared, replaced by the serious expression of the physician. She leans forward in her chair, giving extra emphasis to her next sentence.

"Why do you want to see a psychiatrist, Mr. Fodor?"

The melodious voice, the perfect diction and looks: she should have been an actress, I am thinking. She speaks far better than most actresses I've directed.

I am expecting her question, but I am unprepared. Shall I play along for awhile until an auspicious moment presents itself to reveal my true intention—whatever that is—or, shall I just blurt it out now? If I tell her now that I am obsessed with her, with her image, that she reminds me of a girl I knew forty years ago, she'll throw me out of her office. In the past I've met some girls and women who reminded me of Marika in certain small ways but not to such remarkable degree. They didn't reach me the way Cass Atwill did instantaneously. Can it be, I wonder, that my quest for this particular woman is nothing more than a wish to fall in love? Is it that rapturous moment that interests me, the slow crystallization process, as Stendhal put it, that blinds the lover to reality? Theorizing is useless in matters of love; it never changes one's feelings.

I must come up with an answer quickly but her eyes, her commanding presence paralyze my thinking. She is growing suspicious of my silence. I cannot tell her an outright lie, but I'll give her some half-truths that will free me from talking about myself.

I put my palms together and rest my chin on them pretending to look introspective. It feels good and I am certain it appears contemplative to a shrink. After a short while I raise my head and look straight into her eyes; I want to suggest strength and honesty.

"I came to see you . . . because I am bothered by my pursuit of unrealistic dreams and goals. It seems to me that I live, intentionally, in a world of unreality that I've created. I don't seem to have the capacity to draw a distinct line between reality and unreality, and I am not using the word unreality as a synonym for illusion. Illusion is intangible, a product of fantasy; it's closer to daydreaming. Unreality, on the other hand, is tangible; it becomes real under certain conditions to the individual experiencing it, or can be perfectly real to another person while at the same time it's unreal to me."

I take a short pause to catch my breath. "Some time in the past my actions looked courageous to me, and to the people around me, and they were indeed. But upon reflection, they may have been the result of unrealistic dreams."

I was watching her carefully as I spoke. She's been attentive throughout my long-winded answer to her simple question. I am not sure what I said but I feel good about it. I believe I am appearing to her as an honest patient who pours out his soul. But I must be careful. If I come across as completely honest this time, what is she going to think of me when I reveal my true purpose for being here? She'll say I'm a good liar but a bad person. The fact is, so far, I haven't actually lied.

I realize that I am staring into her eyes.

"Would you give me an example?" I hear her interrupting my reveries.

"An example?" I repeat her question like a student who's been called upon but doesn't have a clue as to what the right answer is.

"Well," I begin, and pause. "During the Nazi occupation . . . in Hungary . . . I was approximately ten years old then . . . I believed, in fact, I was convinced, that I wouldn't be hurt despite all the horror stories I'd heard from my mother and the people around me. It was unrealistic, even for a child of that age, to be so convinced of his invulnerability while experiencing the brutalities of the Nazis firsthand. It wasn't just hope on my part . . . I wasn't hoping–I knew. I firmly believed then that good prevails and evil is only temporary. You see . . . illusion is an intellectual deceit, whereas unreality is reality yet unfulfilled."

I stop for a few seconds hoping that she will interrupt me, that I won't have to continue. But she remains silent, motionless, like a frame of a broken film stuck in the projector before it melts from the hot light.

Now that I've started, I actually don't mind talking. In fact, I feel compelled to talk. I want her to know about me, my miserable childhood, the war and German occupation, everything that will help create sympathy for myself. It is like being on a first date: you want to tell all about yourself quickly to impress the girl and get on with the serious business of lovemaking.

"A month before my father returned unexpectedly from the forced labor camp to take us into hiding, my mother heard about a place that took in Jewish children, protecting them under the aegis of the Swedish government. At first, I refused to go. I didn't want to be separated from my mother—not only for my own sake as an insecure child, but for her sake too. I didn't want her to be alone. I believed if I were with her she'd survive by virtue of my invulnerability. I was so certain that omnipotent powers were protecting me and my loved ones, that I resolved not to go. But my mother kept insisting. If I stayed in the ghetto with her, she argued, we'd both end up in a concentration camp. She believed that the children's home was safer for me—at least I would have a chance.

"Before we left, my mother slipped a can of sardines into my pocket, probably the only treasure left in our possession. She always had something hidden that she produced in the event of grave emergency. We set out for that protected haven on a rainy day in October, the worst month of the season in Hungary, especially if you didn't have any heating facilities. Most revolutions break out in October, never in sunshine. Have you noticed?" I ask her. She registers my question with an infinitesimal movement of her facial muscles. I continue my story.

"My mother and I walked to that place, a high school converted to a makeshift hostel, not too far from the ghetto where we were forced to move from our apartment. My mother and I didn't say a word to each other until we got there but I detected in her eyes the pain, the knowledge that she might never see me again. She kissed me and told me to watch out for myself. Then she handed me over to a woman, a teacher, maybe, who led me into a large room full of children.

"It was a gutted classroom converted to a dormitory. I didn't believe for a moment I was going to stay in that place full of strangers without my mother.

The new environment unsettled me powerfully. How could such a dreadful thing happen to me?—to me who was supposed to be protected by his guardian angel?—I kept asking myself."

I stop my story again for a minute to think about some of the events and feelings of that particular day. She hasn't moved or changed expression since I started talking. As my eyes wander from her frozen visage I notice a small microphone on her desk aimed at me. So that's why she isn't taking notes, those days are over. She records every word I say so she can quote me verbatim in her next book as an interesting case history, a person suffering from obsessive/compulsive neurosis. I look at my watch. I still have time to wrap up my story. Why doesn't she react to anything I say? I should know better. Shrinks are not supposed to react; they just absorb.

"The next thing I remember," I continue, "is that I was lying on the floor on a small blanket among fifty or sixty kids—mostly my age. I couldn't sleep. I was hungry, restless, and heartbroken. Then suddenly I remembered my treasured can of sardines and decided to open it. I couldn't eat the dinner they served in the evening. It had been a vile smelling yellow pea soup that the woman who'd checked me in had carried into the room in a pail just like the ones used for washing floors. The association with dirt and filth, not to mention the offensive smell, turned my stomach. So I declined my first dinner away from home. The pungent smell of the fish woke up the kid next to me; I offered him some sardines without hesitation. We gobbled up the entire can without bread and pretended to go to sleep. I was restless for awhile but the process of digestion must have helped me finally doze off."

I glance up to meet Dr. Atwill's attentive gaze. She is not faking her interest and empathy, I can tell. Perhaps empathy is an overstatement at this point but she definitely seems to be absorbed in my story.

"I remember I was suddenly wide awake, but wasn't disoriented the way people are who find themselves waking up in a strange bed in a strange place. It was quiet in the dorm. Kids don't make noises when asleep. I must have made the decision to escape in my sleep because the moment I awoke, I was aware of my plan. It's possible that I made the decision when my mother left me there.

"I didn't even attempt to escape through the main entrance. Like a somnambulist who knows instinctively the way, I headed straight to the back door and out into the garden. An inner voice guided me to freedom through the unfamiliar topography. The garden was separated from the street by a tall, wrought-iron fence; it was easy for a skinny kid like me to slip between the bars. I ran and ran until I got home.

"When I entered the apartment, out of breath and exhausted emotionally, my mother hugged me and kissed me. She didn't look surprised. For a long while she didn't say a word about the whole affair. She was crying a lot those days."

I stop talking but keep my eyes on Dr. Atwill. She is still attentive though a little sad. The story must have affected her. Or could I be projecting my own emotions?

"Now, do you think escaping from the hostel was a realistic thing to do?" I ask her in an indignant manner. She doesn't reply immediately; she is not the type who makes statements without careful deliberation.

"It's easier to understand our actions," she answers in a cool, pragmatic manner, "if you break them down into instinct and reason, rather than reality and unreality. In my opinion, instinct is more reliable in terms of survival than reason. Of course, I am talking about the individual, strictly the individual."

In an unexpected change of tone, she asks me softly, almost wistfully, "But what happened to those children in the hostel? Have you ever found out?" I take a deep breath before answering her question. The memory, still vivid, makes me shiver, makes me angry and frustrated.

"The day after I escaped, the Hungarian Fascists raided the place and took all the children to the Danube. They lined them up along the river bank and shot them into the water." I answered flatly to avoid melodramatic effects, and to hide my upsurging emotions.

She falters. "How did you find out about it?"

"My mother heard it from the person who recommended the place. And after the liberation, there was a great deal of talk about this incident. There were a few survivors who weren't badly wounded in the machine-gun fire and who were able to swim to shore."

She doesn't say anything. I also keep quiet, enjoying the silence. Then Dr. Atwill changes position in her chair and adopts a more official demeanor.

"This . . . reality versus unreality conflict . . . Does it make you suffer to such a degree that you have to seek help, or are there other problems as well that are contributing to your self-diagnosed neurosis?"

How can she be so sarcastic, so collected, right after hearing my story? But what do I expect? She is a shrink, after all. It's her job to be objective. She listens to horror stories all day; it's surprising that she is actually sane—maybe she isn't, how do I know?

But how shall I answer her question? She is expecting a coherent and intelligent response that proves my neurosis, that justifies my hundred-dollar-an-hour visit. She is an honest shrink, she won't rip me off for all that money without some conviction of an existing problem. Or at least a mild form of mental illness.

I wonder how much time is left of my session. I want to look at my watch but don't want to appear rude, so I sneak a quick look and hope she doesn't notice. My time is nearly up but there is still enough left for a short statement to whet her appetite. I can't let her dismiss me or I'll lose her for good.

Like a student who suddenly remembers the solution to an Euclidean theorem, I blurt out the words.

"I also have an obsession that's getting out of hand. I have difficulties in controlling it . . . "

"What sort of obsession?" she interrupts me. She is clever. She must have noticed that I looked at my watch; she must have sensed my rising anxiety.

"It's . . . it's sexual in nature, but it's not what you think, it's not obvious at all . . . " I had put my foot into my mouth again.

"I didn't try to guess what it could be," she interrupts again. "But go on, please!"

I don't know where to start. I look at my watch, this time openly. "I am exhausted. I am not used to this. Perhaps, I'll tell you about it next time?"

"All right, Mr. Fodor. I'll see you day after tomorrow, same time."

I become conscious of sweat running down the inside of my arm—I can even smell it. I am wondering if she does too? As we shake hands, I stay as far away from her as I can.

We exchange polite smiles and I leave her office by a door that leads directly out to the corridor. For a moment I am disoriented by the shortcut. It is an exhausting but exhilarating charade I am playing with her. It makes me nervous but I can't help being thrilled about the prospect of making love to her, falling in love with her, spending the rest of my life with her.

* * *

IV.

AT FIRST, I flatly refused when my mother asked me to bring up coal from the basement. She vowed to tell my father that I didn't obey her. But I knew he would do nothing. He was interested in party politics, not domestic affairs. As soon as we were liberated by the Red Army, he joined the Communist Party.

Then my mother threatened to deny my allowance for a week. This didn't bother me either because all my money came from my father and I was able to manipulate him better than my mother ever could. As a last resort, she swore that she would withhold walnut cookies and all desserts for the rest of the week. That did it.

Our building didn't have a central heating system. That was the privilege of the rich who could afford to buy the condominiums overlooking the Danube, built in the late thirties. In our modest flat, one large coal stove heated the living room and the master bedroom. A small stove heated the common room that was both the gathering place of the family during the day and my brother's bedroom at night before he was taken to a forced labor camp and subsequently to an Austrian concentration camp.

My grandfather and I fought continually for the chair next to the little stove. It was his favorite place for an afternoon snooze and mine for reading during the damp winter days.

Being the youngest in the family, I got assigned the chores nobody else wanted to do, such as lugging ice in the summer from the corner vendor, or carrying up coal in the winter from our locker in the basement. I dreaded these duties. I was afraid of the darkness and the large spiders hiding in every corner, and the giant cockroaches that came out every night and ran up the staircase, trying to find their way into the apartments. Only a small electric bulb lit the stairs to the basement; beyond that it was a black hole. The candle I carried with me barely lit the space in front of my nose and I might easily walk into a cobweb.

Also, the basement brought back memories of my nightly tortures in the air-raid shelter, the family huddled together, listening to the explosions of chain-bombs from the Allied air attacks, waiting for our imminent death. During those moments of terror, not even the prayers to my guardian angel could ease my anxiety. I still hate spiders and cockroaches, and the dark.

The day we moved back to our cherished apartment, my father and I secretly went down to our basement locker.

"Not on the first day!" I cried out in my mind. Why is he dragging me down to that awful place, ruining this wonderful moment of being at home finally? We should celebrate our survival, rejoice that our apartment is intact, that our belongings are saved.

My father instructed me to hold the candle.

"Can't mother hold the candle?" I protested.

"No, I don't want to draw the neighbors' attention to us," he said. No one will pay attention to you and me going down to the basement, he argued.

Inside the locker, I stood with the candle in my hand and watched as my father shoveled the coal from one place to another and dug up the earth at a spot he had cleared of coal. He worked feverishly, like a grave robber. Then his shovel stopped. He bent down and lifted out from the small hole a dark, heavy metal box. I watched him, all my fears slowly vanishing. The Nazis were defeated, the Allies had stopped bombing, life was going to be wonderful from now on, except for the spiders.

The small, golden coins, with Napoleon's head on one side were brand new. The dollar bills, all green, were used, held together by a rubber band. The jewelry was familiar; I recognized my mother's solid gold bracelets and my father's gold pocket watch. All the family's fortune was contained in that little black box. My mother cried with joy when we brought it up to her. Had someone else found our treasure, we'd have been left without a penny, completely destitute.

Next day, after we had finished putting all the furniture back in exactly the position it had been in—under my mother's supervision—on that day in 1922 when my brother was born, my father decided that we should leave Budapest for a while until the Germans were pushed back further west. He didn't want to take chances in case the Germans recaptured the city—a real possibility in the ongoing tug of war. I loathed the idea of leaving so soon after settling back in our place. I felt perfectly safe in my old bed. Also, that girl behind the kitchen window haunted my imagination; I wanted to meet her.

With heavy hearts we packed a few essentials and left for the railway station which, ironically, had survived the war. On our way out of the building I tried to catch a glimpse of Marika, but she wasn't at the window.

The train was full of drab, unwashed, miserable-looking people—all on the run from the city in fear of the Nazis' return. During the entire trip we had to stand in the tightly packed compartment.

I had never been to Szeged before. It is a moderately- sized city famous in the west for its sweet, red paprika. We checked into the best hotel in town which, to our surprise, was open to guests and had suffered no damage in the war. Thank God my father liked traveling first class. It seemed, when we arrived, that we were the only guests. This beautiful mini-grand hotel with its limited, sleepy staff and a few dining patrons was a bizarre sight even for a child. I enjoyed the serenity, the lack of people and crowds, and the sudden relief from danger. Though my parents didn't articulate it to me I knew they felt the same way I did.

My mother and father got bored after a few days without friends or work. We didn't know anybody in the city and there was nothing to do but play gin rummy all day and wait for the German army to be far enough from Budapest to return home and live in safety.

Every day we ate in the hotel's splendid dining room which offered only turkey soup with pieces of white meat floating on the surface. I hated turkey;

it is an ugly bird to eat. It took me days and lots of convincing before I was willing to touch the soup; I lived on bread and nuts. Only days before, I'd eaten horsemeat. But now that threat to my life was over, I became a fussy eater again.

I longed to go back to school, to be with my friends, or to make new friends. I had finished elementary school and had no idea if any of my schoolmates would be going to the same high school I was, or even if they had survived the war.

I was thinking of Marika a lot. She would be a perfect mate for me since she lived in the same building. My curiosity about girls preoccupied me all day. Girls were a great mystery for me; there were none in our family.

I am not certain how long we stayed in Szeged. All I recall is the ennui, the relentless boredom we all had to endure.

I don't recall a spring so wonderful and so full of promise as the one in 1945. The war was practically over, we were free from Nazi persecution and I was going to my first year of *gymnasium*, the equivalent of junior high in the United States. I was thrilled by the new subjects in school–particularly Latin. In those days you needed Latin to enter the university to study law, medicine and the humanities. Learning that ancient language, full of implied mysteries and secret knowledge, made me feel I already belonged to a privileged class of people.

Since it was a Jewish gymnasium, I had to study Hebrew as well, and Judaism. I wasn't too fond of the Hebrew language; it was too guttural and alien to me. Also, I didn't see the sense of studying one more ancient language since all the other gymnasiums in the city only required one. But in order to protect me from anti-Semite bullies, my parents insisted that I go to a religious school. I didn't think I would have to worry about anti-Semitism in those days right after the Nazis were defeated. It is not that the sentiment wasn't there, deep-seated, but now it was dangerous and illegal to express it openly.

I wasn't too happy about the religious services I had to attend every Saturday either. I only believed in my personal guardian angel, not in a God who created the universe and mankind. I had seen too much human suffering to believe in an omnipotent God and, at that time, being young and ignorant, I didn't see the enormous significance Judaism has and has always had in the life of the Jewish people.

For weeks after our return from Szeged, I was hoping to cross paths with Marika. One day while I assisted my mother in the kitchen—I loved watching her bake—I asked her about the new family downstairs, hoping she had met Marika's mother. She told me that they were Gypsies and the little girl was their stepdaughter. From her description of Marika's parents, I realized that I had seen her stepmother a few times on my way home from school. She was a good-looking woman in her early thirties with jet-black hair and fiery eyes. She had even smiled at me once with innocent provocation.

One sunny day in April, the most beautiful month of the year in Hungary, I was coming home from school, strolling along the busy streets, alone, wallowing in a rotten mood. I hadn't performed well in Latin class. I'd had a strep throat the week before, missed more than a week of school and hadn't caught up with all my homework.

As I crossed the courtyard I saw her immediately. Marika was sitting in the wide open kitchen window with a book in her hand. I stopped without hesitation. We greeted each other as if we were old friends and she asked me if I wanted to come in.

Being on street level their apartment was dark and depressing. I was instantly put off by the new, unfamiliar smell, the sunless rooms, the unsettling mood of the place. I sensed privation everywhere.

Marika wore her blonde hair in a ponytail. She was obviously not a Gypsy. I didn't think about this incongruity until I saw her in the apartment standing next to her stepmother. Perhaps, I thought innocently, her stepparents stole her from some farmer's house in the country before coming to Budapest.

Marika was lively and direct, a real busybody, asking endless questions about me and my family, and school. I realized she knew a great deal about us through her stepmother, who was a gossip. I was relaxed and comfortable in her company. She behaved with wonderful ease considering this was the first time we had met. Of course, it is easy for children—they haven't learned enough about life, about relationships to be inhibited—and she was older than I. Soon after we exchanged the obligatory information about each other, I asked her if she wanted to go for a walk in the City Park that afternoon. She agreed eagerly.

I floated home. It was the first time in my life that I experienced such

z

feeling, such joy: a beautiful girl is interested in walking with me in the park. When my mother saw me she immediately knew that something had happened to me. I was excited and bubbly, and asked her to serve my lunch at once. When she inquired why the big hurry, I told her matter-of-factly that I had a date with Marika Toth, the Gypsies' stepdaughter. She said, without missing a beat, that Marika was much too old for me and I should stay at home to study. I didn't argue with her. I sensed that her response was the obvious one for a concerned mother and was not to be taken too seriously. It wasn't in the Hungarian tradition for parents to object to their sons' dating habits, as long as they involved the opposite sex. The earlier dating started, the prouder they were, without admitting it.

After I gobbled up my lunch, which wasn't much—food was still scarce in those days—I blasted out of the apartment before my mother could ask where I was going. We lived on the second floor of a three-story building without an elevator. City kids learned at a very young age to race down staircases in old apartment buildings, jumping two steps at a time; it was perfected to an art form. We used to set up races in school during recess and make bets. Some of us developed the skill to such a degree that we actually slid down the stairs without actually making any distinct steps, except at the landings where you had to turn. That is how I approached Marika's apartment on the main floor.

I rang the doorbell impatiently until Mrs. Toth opened the door. I was disappointed that Marika wasn't alone, but Mrs. Toth's friendly smile disarmed me. She invited me inside and yelled to Marika at the back of the apartment that I had arrived and was waiting. Marika ran out of their bedroom dressed in a blue skirt and white blouse, looking angelic with her blonde hair tied with blue ribbons. Her stepmother was delighted to see us off; she must have believed that her stepdaughter was safe with me.

The City Park in Budapest is as large and popular as Central Park in New York City or the Bois de Boulogne in Paris, and it was only a ten-minute walk from where we lived.

As soon as we stepped out of the building Marika took my hand and didn't let it go until we reached the playgrounds in the park. Her hand was warm and comforting but also troubling. No girl had ever held my hand for such a long stretch of time. During our walk I kept wondering why she hung onto me with such determination. I considered the possibility that being older than I, she perhaps wanted to practice motherhood on me. But I was eleven years old, not a toddler. Soon I came to the conclusion that it was just a friendly gesture; she probably wanted to treat me as a mate.

The City Park provided recreation facilities for both young and old: if you were in a romantic or foolish mood you could rent a boat on the large, artificial lake surrounded by willow and acacia trees. There were ballparks to play soccer, Hungary's most popular sport, playgrounds with swings and sandboxes for kids and forests for hiking. The park was a haven for old men and women, young couples in love, children, and for truants who would rather play soccer than learn a Pythagorean theorem. You could play chess on park benches or hide in the bushes with your girlfriend. I spent a considerable amount of time there in my youth.

By the time Marika and I arrived most of the swings and moving contraptions were crowded. It was a perfect spring day and it appeared that everyone in the whole city had decided to escape from their drab apartments to take in some sun and fresh air.

As we strolled among the parents and kids Marika noticed two boys getting off one of the seesaws. We dashed to it and eagerly climbed on at each end, carefully balancing, and began to move up and down with increasing speed.

Soon, her short skirt slipped up on her legs and stayed that way, giving me a perfect view of her pink panties as she kept her legs apart to encircle the wooden seat. My eyes were glued to the sight. Not having seen female genitalia, I was painfully curious about what was behind those panties. In school we talked about sex and sex organs incessantly but only a few kids had really seen a naked girl. I was mesmerized by the pink spot as she made the seesaw move higher and higher, up and down, laughing and shrieking in the process.

I began to feel dizzy. At one point my end of the seesaw hit the ground and I fell off the seat, sending her side down unexpectedly. She also fell off but didn't hurt herself. She ran to my rescue and checked out my legs and arms and held my head for a while, though not with serious concern. She just played the role of my protector.

We didn't talk about the incident on our way home. Instead of holding my hand, this time she put her arm around my shoulder, like boys used to do in Hungary with their best friends on their way to a forbidden destination. Her closeness gave me an unusual headache, but at the same time, I wanted her to hold me. A pleasant new smell emanated from her hair, a mixture of shampoo and the scent of her fair skin. It added to my torture and pleasure. These sensations were new to me and I may not have been ready for them.

I was flushed and feverish by the time I got home. My mother cleaned up my bruises and poured iodine on them and insisted that I take an aspirin and go to bed. She didn't scold me or ask questions; she knew perfectly well what had happened to me.

Since Hungarian high schools at the time were separated into boys' and girls' buildings, we didn't have direct contact with the opposite sex in the classroom. That system prevented us from developing healthy relationships with girls and also from opportunities to date. Victorian sexual mores still prevailed.

My best friend in school was Irvin, a sweet-natured, shy but intelligent boy. He was fat and the butt of pranksters. I was skinny, dreamy and aloof—with little interest in the normal activities of school programs.

Irvin lived a block away from us on the same street. Every morning I picked him up and we walked to school together. I had a whistle signal to herald my arrival: the first two measures of "Yankee Doodle Dandy". Truthfully, it was the signal of my brother's gang but I liked the tune and the movie. Irvin and I became known as "the Skinny and the Fat".

We had one binding characteristic in common: neither of us was any good at sports. That alone was enough for a deep and lasting friendship to take hold.

My interest in girls developed sooner than Irvin's, a fact that created conflicts and periodical breaks in our friendship. His sexual awakening began at fifteen when he met a chubby girl at a school dance. He stayed with her throughout his studies and after medical school they got married. My sexual adventures were stormier, and my curiosity about women has been insatiable all my life.

Fortunately, my curiosity extended to the sciences as well. I became interested in electronics and spent every spare moment building wirelesses and reading books on the subject I didn't understand.

Marika and electronics occupied my fantasies. I didn't care much about anything else. I perfunctorily studied the required subjects in school but they didn't interest me as much as physics and math. At that time, literature and poetry bored me. All I wanted was to become a scientist and marry Marika.

* * *

V.

THE SANTA ANA winds are still blowing hot, dry air in from the desert.

I wake up in the middle of the night with a dry throat and burning membranes; I can't swallow or breathe through my nose. When I switch on the bedside lamp I notice right away that I forgot to fill up the humidifier.

I get out of bed and saunter into the kitchen to drink some water–lots of water. As I fill the tank of my high-tech humidifier I can't help wondering how people lived for thousands of years in the desert without it. I suppose they didn't live long lives–except for the prophets.

I don't sleep well these days and the reason for my restless nights is not only the desert winds. It's also anxiety. Whenever I am between films, a Hollywood euphemism for being out of work, I am hit with an anxiety attack. My last four films didn't make money. Consequently, I am mistrusted by the distributors and won't be redeemed until I approach them with a screenplay they badly want to do.

My agent keeps sending me schlock scripts, referred to in the industry as "genre stuff," but I turn them down. I would rather direct TV movies than waste my time and energy on idiotic theatrical feature films.

I have too much time on my hands right now—too much time to contemplate my past, the mistakes I've made, the future. I am surprised I can sleep at all. When I don't work, my sexual fantasies take over my imagination and my obsessions surface. Only serious work can keep a healthy balance between reality and unreality.

It was not my dry throat that woke me up just now; it was a nightmare. Truthfully, it wasn't a conventional nightmare, since it ended with an erotic dream complete with surrealistic imagery. Every time I sleep on my left side I suffer bad dreams, on my back I experience erotic dreams. But this time I was on my right side, so my dreams must have been caused by the Santa Ana winds combined with the anxiety of a film director waiting for his next project.

I dreamt that as a child I was in the Second World War, driving a tank in the front lines. The gas tank got hit and burst into a ball of fire. I desperately tried to escape but couldn't open the overhead hatch. The heat became unbearable. I began to suffocate and gasp for air. Then, just before I blacked out, I realized I was now in Dr. Atwill's office. I was lying on the leather couch and her secretary was methodically undressing me, touching my nakedness periodically with slow, erotic movements of her hand. I didn't like her doing it at the beginning but then she became such an expert at it that I stopped resisting. She kept repeating that the doctor wanted to conduct her session with me while I was nude. When she reached my underpants, her true finesse revealed itself. She slowly rolled down my shorts, squatted to have easier access and placed me into her mouth. At that moment I woke up with a parched throat.

I turn off the tap in the kitchen and carry the water tank into my bedroom. I am still under the influence of my dream as I slip back under the sheet, too tired to analyze it though I still feel its residual unpleasantness. I judge my dreams by the mood they leave behind. Often, this mood remains with me for the rest of the day.

I can't go back to sleep. I keep thinking about Cass Atwill.

When I enter Dr. Atwill's office, she doesn't point to the chair I occupied on my first visit but to the couch placed strategically in a corner of the room near her desk.

"Make yourself comfortable, Mr. Fodor. You'll find it easier to concentrate and talk about yourself in a reclining position," she says as casual as only a shrink can be who knows she is in control of the situation and her patient.

"I am not so convinced about it but I'll try," I say, knowing that I am going to hate it. I have always wondered why some people are so enthusiastic about seeing analysts, talking willingly about their pasts and secrets to a stranger while lying on their backs.

As soon as I lie down I realize that I am not looking at her anymore. My head faces a wall of books across from her desk. I presume she doesn't want the patients staring at her and being distracted by her during the sessions. I'll go along with this inconvenience today, I say to myself, but next time I'll insist on a chair facing her.

"On your last visit you spoke about a sexual obsession affecting you to such degree that you were compelled to seek professional help. Will you elaborate on it a little more?" she asks me with her controlled professionalism. I hate gazing at the wall; I want to see her face, although it may turn out to be easier to lie through my teeth if I'm not facing her.

"When I was eleven years old," I begin, "I fell in love with a thirteen year old girl who lived in our building. Over the years I watched her grow up and get married. Ever since the first time I saw her I've been fantasizing about her. Whenever I make love her image pops into my mind. I feel terribly guilty about deceiving all the women I've loved in my youth and adult life. I want to get rid of this image; I want to wipe her face out of my memory; I want to create *tabula rasa* in my mind. That's the reason I came to see you." I stop and wait for her next question. It isn't coming. I raise my torso and turn to see if she has fallen asleep or left the office, but she is still there fossilized at her desk, staring at me like a Hindu snake charmer.

"Aren't you going to ask me more questions?" I hesitantly encourage her.

"Not yet," she says emphatically, "just keep on talking, or stay silent if you wish." Sure, that would be the easiest way to make money—just listening to the long silences of the patients. A wonderful way to cure someone's neurosis: healing by osmosis. What shall I talk about? I don't want to tell her yet that she is the one who could cure me by fucking me, that she is the one who looks like Marika, and that I want her badly. When am I going to tell her that, I keep asking myself. I am mute. Soon I will fall asleep.

"Most people fantasize about a third person while making love. I wouldn't consider that neurotic behavior in itself." Her voice, this time softer than before, brings me back from the threshold of sleep.

"It's more than just a sexual turn-on for me," I reply without thinking. "I believe I missed out on something important because I didn't act the way I should have when the opportunities were still there." I stop again. It is painful to think about the past. Lately, I have been too preoccupied with my childhood; it is part of the aging process, I suppose. I am looking back to reassess the mistakes I have made in order to feel miserable about them. The career mistakes don't bother me as much as the personal ones.

There is a long silence again.

It is becoming worse than a dinner party when conversation comes to a halt and the pressure is on the host to rescue the evening. On those occasions, I often throw in a time bomb—make a derogatory statement about militant feminism, for example. The conversation suddenly comes alive and the evening is saved. At the end of the party I apologize and confess to my manipulation but the guests seldom believe me.

What shall I tell her before the odious silence floods my armpits?

"Mr. Fodor . . . " I hear my name flying at me with such portent that my body jerks on the couch as if I have just had an electric shock. Was it the tone of her voice, or the inflection of her reading, or both? I don't like it at all. It sounds suspiciously inquisitive. I am afraid of where it will lead. "Why have you chosen me as your psychiatrist? Who recommended me to you?" Not one, but two disturbing questions.

I knew it was coming, she is too smart not to bring it up. I must tell her the truth; I have had enough of this charade. Slowly, I rise from the couch and walk over to her desk. I take the chair which I occupied on my first visit and sit facing her. She leans into her high-back executive chair expecting a confession. I think I detect a tiny smirk on her face. There's been too much pressure on me lately, too much reflection on the past—I am drifting again. I need a vacation soon. Normally, I don't take them. I travel a lot when I am in production. Either the film is shot on location, or after it is completed and turns out well, I take it to film festivals. I enjoy vacations better when they're paid for by producers. But, where was I? Oh, yes. I am about to make a statement. I must drop the sickly expression I put on when I entered her office. There is no time left for continuing the deceit. The jig is up. I have to be honest with her. I make a pathetic attempt to turn on my charm, whatever is left of it after years of abuse in Hollywood. I smile at her as if we were in a restaurant drinking champagne to our budding relationship.

"I am going to answer your second question first. Nobody recommended you. I have found you on my own." I notice she raises her eyebrows. They are well shaped. She must pluck them herself every week. They are not the same shade as her hair; she must darken them too.

"You don't really want a psychiatrist at all, do you?" comes the question I have been expecting all along. I must be awfully careful of my next move. I decide an honest confession will impress her most.

"A few days ago, I saw you on the street and followed you to your office," I say as calmly as I can. "You look exactly like Marika, the girl whose image obsesses me."

She listens attentively—probably contemplates calling the police. She could have a secret button under her desk which she has already activated. Help is on the way. The police will harass me, or even arrest me; I'll be on the eleven o'clock news; my career is over.

"I hope you don't find my actions out of line. How could I resist the temptation? I've been waiting for this moment for years, decades. I couldn't afford to let the opportunity pass."

She listens without any evidence of compassion or anger. Perhaps I am on the right track.

"For me, it's normal to pursue women. It may not be the American way, but I can't reject my heritage . . . "

"Do you really believe that having intercourse with me will cure you of your obsession?" She interrupts me, then tilts her head, as if she were addressing a five-year-old. She laughs out loud. She didn't say *making love*. The word *intercourse* is more scientific, more medical. After all, we are talking about curing someone sick in the head.

"Intercourse wouldn't do," I say calmly. I am convinced now she won't call the police. "Only lovemaking would do the job." She laughs out loud again, but this time her voice wavers a bit. I sense she doesn't know what to do or say next.

"What if I don't share your feelings?" She asks after some deliberation.

"It's against psychiatric practice to get involved emotionally with patients." She is obviously stalling. She thinks my time will be up soon and I will have to leave without arguments, and she will instruct her secretary not to let me into her office ever again.

"You're quite presumptuous, Mr. Fodor. I advise you to see another psychiatrist, perhaps a male this time . . . " I interrupt her with an edge in my voice.

"I am not interested in seeing a psychiatrist! It was a coincidence that you turned out to be one. I wish you were a stockbroker, or a film producer. Yes, that would've been perfect. We would've had a lot to talk about. I would've tried to pitch you one of my stories, the one nobody wants to finance in this town. Yes, that would've been perfect." She smiles again—I think to calm me down.

"Since we have only a few minutes left, let us try to resolve the situation. I suggest we simply forget this encounter altogether and that you seek help elsewhere."

"But you must understand, I am not sick!" I protest. She keeps smiling as if to suggest I need a straightjacket, not a lover. "I didn't want to see a shrink, I wanted to meet you." I stop for a second. I am not sure I should tell her how I feel about her, that I love her, that it was love at first sight. She'll be scared and I won't be able to see her ever again.

"As I said before, under these conditions I can't continue the therapy. I'm sorry." Therapy? I am not sick. Her words sound final, but not her delivery—she left some vague hope there, I am sure. It is not my imagination. The subtext wasn't completely negative. I can tell. That's exactly what I watch for in a good performance on the set—the subtext. I must push her further, if I give up now I'll never see her again.

"If you refuse to see me professionally in your office why don't you have lunch with me, at least once?"

"I don't see the point of it." She takes a quick glance at her watch and looks up at me. "Your time is up, Mr. Fodor." She rises and extends her hand smiling at the same time, either out of politeness or compassion, or—shall I believe it?— a feeling of emerging interest, or perhaps more. I do the same. The palm of her hand is soft and warm, and she lets me hold it long enough to suggest some unconscious encouragement to carry with me.

On my way out I stop at the door, just the way I would stage it in a scene for a movie, and blurt out my exit line. "I'll see you tomorrow for lunch. One o'clock in the Bistro Garden." I leave before she can say no.

I feel much better. I can be myself now, no more of this putting-on-an-act nonsense. As I descend in the elevator of Dr. Atwill's office building I look at myself in the mirror and realize instantly that I have embarked again on an unrealistic venture. Why am I compelled to act that way? Every major move in my life has been unrealistic. My friends, even my parents when they were still alive, warned me against my actions but I never listened. I just forge ahead toward a projected goal blithely disregarding the obstacles ahead. Am I out of my mind, or just a firm believer in doing the thing I imagine I must do?

The elevator stops and a few worried-looking patients enter. Their uncomfortable presence interrupts my thought process for a fraction of a second.

Do I really regret most of the important actions I took throughout the years? What was my first unrealistic move? Well, how far back shall I go? Perhaps the Hungarian Revolution is far enough. Emigration is never a realistic or smart move for a creative person unless it is vital for his physical survival. When I left Hungary in 1956 it wasn't for that; it was for the survival of my spirit. I wanted to make films in the West; I wanted to enjoy free artistic expression. Little did I know at the time that, film being an expensive art form, I still wouldn't enjoy the degree of freedom I craved, not even in the West.

It wasn't strictly the Stalinist regime that induced me to leave Hungary; I never felt quite at home there after the war. My childhood experiences under the Nazis didn't stop haunting me. The specter of anti-Semitism continued to exist. I was uprooted there before I was born. I hope, one day, I will find my roots.

As I step out of the medical building I am halted by the intense, harsh light. I reach for my sunglasses but not even those extra-dark lenses can relieve the pain in my eyes.

At once I discover that I am without a specific destination or purpose. I flatly refuse to go home and sit at my desk. I much prefer reading at night. The sun doesn't let you stay indoors, it is too seductive, it drives you out of your house. That's why people on the East Coast look down on Californians as illiterate flakes. We do not have enough rainy days when we are happy to stay at home and do some serious thinking and work.

It is five o'clock. Perhaps I should have a drink. But I only drink in the company of friends. Actually, I need a drink badly right now.

I walk up to a public phone and call Phoebe. She picks up the phone on the first ring like an actress who has been out of work for years, waiting for her agent to return her call.

"Oh, hi. It's you?" she bubbles. "I didn't expect *you* to call this time of the day. Don't you normally call at night when you want to get laid?"

I am still thrown by Phoebe's bluntness and vulgarity.

"Well, don't exaggerate! We had lunches once in a while and movies at night, without sex."

"Why don't I remember those days?" she says giggling at the other end.

"Anyway, would you join me for a drink?"

"All right. Where are you?"

"How about the Polo Lounge? It's right next door to you." She hangs up without telling me how long it will take her to get ready. I love her style, I envy her freedom and egotistical outlook on the world, her natural brazenness that defers to only a few. How did she become that way? Her money and upbringing? I doubt it. Her parents are subdued compared to her, she couldn't have inherited her temperament from them. Must be the grandparents, or else the lucky combination of millions of previously insignificant genetic factors. Phoebe is what is known to Europeans as the quintessential *American girl.*

I like the Polo Lounge in the Beverly Hills Hotel for its quiet, civilized ambiance. I could've suggested Cafe Roma, where you can sit for hours sipping an espresso, watching the pretty girls go by—very European. But after my session with Dr. Atwill I feel the need for a bar with low-key lighting and suppressed conversations around tables. I am emotionally drained, like after a difficult day of shooting a film. Working with actors is not unlike seducing a woman, and I am certain with Dr. Atwill it will come to a long and arduous seduction game. I am the one who is in love. She doesn't share my emotion at the moment—at least that's what she demonstrates to me.

The bar is tranquil now, less than half full, but soon after the studio executives have returned all their calls for the day it will become crowded and boisterous. I find a peaceful corner and ask the waiter for a Calvados. This is among the few bars in Los Angeles that carry this French apple brandy. Calvados represents for me an early romantic period in my life. I think I was sixteen when I read Erich Maria Remarque's *The Arch of Triumph*. In his favorite watering hole, the hero of the book always asked for a Calvados while waiting for his sweetheart. After I read the book, for a long time I fantasized about Paris and its bars and was hoping to fall in love with a beautiful French girl and drink Calvados with her at the Ritz.

As I sit in anticipation with my eyes half closed, I imagine the wonderful aroma: a mixture of apple and alcohol plus a magical ingredient only nature could create and describe.

The approaching waiter interrupts my musings. He places on the table the apple brandy and some salted nuts that I never touch because they make me thirsty and yet I can't stop eating them. I take a sip of my drink. It burns my throat and stomach. One cannot get a smooth, well-aged Calvados in Los Angeles. Well, this is better than not having any.

I begin to feel better in the air-conditioned room after a few sips of my drink. Phoebe hasn't shown up yet. I keep inhaling the vapor of the brandy while musing about France and Paris, and watching the people arrive for their meetings and dates. It is easy to figure out who is who from their attire. The smooth but scared young studio executives almost always wear hip, black Italian suits; young actors normally fit into tight, worn jeans and shirts; producers are less predictable: it depends on the grosses of their last picture. When they are doing well they buy the same Armani suits as do the studio executives, but they give themselves away with their smile. Producers always smile and pretend to be in great spirits. They must give the impression to the executives that they are happy with the lousy scripts they schlep around all day.

The young starlets dress provocatively. They sell the idea of sex—only the idea, for they are sexless themselves. A tall blonde passes by my table holding the hand of her agent. I recognize his face from one of the large agencies, probably ICM; they used to represent me. She is in skin-tight jeans and a blouse open down to her navel. As she walks by in profile I can see her left breast in full.

Phoebe arrives dressed the same way as the girl who just walked by my table, except her blouse is buttoned up to show only half of her breasts.

"Ciao commandatore," she greets me with a perfect Italian accent. She must be studying Italian Neo-realism in her film history course, or screwing an Italian boy from her class. She kisses me and plunks herself down at the tiny table, then leans over my drink and makes a face suggesting disgust.

"How can you drink this heavy shit when it's a hundred degrees outside?" she asks with her customary directness.

"I needed something strong. What are you going to drink?" The waiter is already hovering over our table.

"A champagne cocktail, please," she demands, as if she were accustomed to drinking one every day during the recesses at USC. Then she turns to me with an impish smile.

"How come you called me in the afternoon? Guys at your age normally fuck in the evening, or in the morning." Older men are her specialty, I think, though she has never bragged to me about it. She must be suffering from a *father fixation.*

"I don't want to make love now. I just wanted to talk to you. Is that OK?" I ask her without any hint of seriousness.

"Sure. What do you want to talk about? Movies, sex, politics?"

"They are all pretty good subjects. In fact, they practically exhaust the areas worth talking about." I have another sip of Calvados. The waiter places Phoebe's drink in front of her. She grabs the glass and knocks back half of the champagne as if it were plain water.

"Why do you date me, Phoebe? You must've thought about it. You're so much younger than I. You should be going out with guys from your class," I say unconvincingly, fishing for compliments.

"Why? Because I'm comfortable with you . . . and I'm ambitious. Eventually, you'll help me in the industry. Unless, of course, you're a cad. But I can read guys, you're a nice one. You'll help me, won't you?" She takes my face in her hands and kisses me on the mouth.

No one can resist the magic and power of flattery when it is delivered with such bluntness. I know she is lying through her teeth, and I know the truths she utters will turn into self-serving lies in the long run, but I believe in her because she is convincing, and I forgive her when I catch her in a lie because I know she's got the psyche of a cat. I think she is an actress manqué.

"Do you realize you're one of the few Jewish girls I've dated? I married shiksas."

'Why is that?" she asks without much interest.

"It's too complicated to get into. I'm exhausted this afternoon. I'll tell you some other time."

"Didn't you just say you wanted to talk? You make little sense today, Gabi." She gulps down her drink and gestures to leave. "Let's go!" she demands with a broad smile. "I hate this place." She leans a few inches toward me and runs her index finger down the ridge of my nose. "I want to fuck you right now. Let's go!"

I pay and we leave. She drags me out of the bar like a mother would pull her obese child out of a candy shop.

"What makes you so horny in the middle of the afternoon?" I ask stupidly on our way out of the hotel. She is twenty-two years old, for God's sake. I keep forgetting.

'Oh, I struggled with a love scene in my script this morning. It's between a young girl and this older guy . . . and it turned me on. You know how you imagine a scene in great detail before you write it? I don't have to tell you that. You know how scripts are written."

"Is the story about you and me?"

She nods. "You're not worried, are you?" She giggles.

"No, not until I read it. Just kidding. Actually, I'm flattered. I hope it's good. Perhaps you want me to direct it?" I say this as a joke but I mean it.

"You're very quick," she replies with some sarcasm. "That's the idea."

As we drive south on Beverly Drive, she puts her left hand on my crotch.

"It's time for some preparatory work, don't you think?"

"I believe it's against the law," I protest, aroused.

"The best things in life are always against something. Didn't you tell me that?"

'Did I?"

"Yes, you did." And she squeezes me hard.

I leave my car with the Chicano valet in front of the building. I never park it myself when I come home with a woman. Women don't like dark garages;

there are too many rapes in the city. Also, it is more civilized to enter a building through the main door and a safe lobby.

A middle-aged couple steps into the elevator just before the door closes on us. I have seen them before. They live on the eighteenth floor. The woman looks older than her husband—an unusual sight in Hollywood—and doesn't hide her disgust at Phoebe's youth and my arrogance at taking a young girl up to my apartment. From the corner of his eyes the husband ogles Phoebe's perfect figure. Wickedly, Phoebe rubs against me, kisses my cheek and runs her hand through my hair. The woman turns away from us with obvious revulsion.

The elevator stops on the fourteenth floor and we step out.

"Have a good one!" the man remarks, as is customary in California. We burst out laughing as the door closes behind us. Phoebe takes my hand and pulls me in a mad dash to my apartment.

I live in a two-bedroom unit densely packed with books, records and videotapes. A large, iron sculpture dominates the living room, a precious present from a well-known Montreal sculptor who worked as a production designer on my first dramatic film in Canada. Phoebe shoots straight to the bedroom and throws herself on the unmade bed.

"Pull my jeans down, quick!" At the same time, she sheds her blouse revealing her beautiful breasts. She never wears a bra. There is a most uncommon aspect to her breasts: just by rubbing or sucking on her nipples, I can bring her to a quick orgasm.

As I look at this wonderful creature in my bed ready to love me, my fantasy cruelly creates images of Marika and Dr. Atwill. I will have to keep my eyes open as we make love, the only way to rid myself of the intruding blondes.

My hand glides over her firm buttocks, up her spine and to her amazing breasts. Her breathing becomes heavier, then rapidly goes out of control. She pulls my head down to one of her nipples. She likes to start this way. My eyes close automatically and I see Marika at the poolside in one of the public baths in Budapest, lying on the suntan lotion-stained concrete in a daisy patterned bikini. She is sixteen and fully developed. I am next to her with my eyes fixed on her breasts and crotch, feeling embarrassed by my skinny, fourteen-year-old body. Then I see Dr. Atwill, behind her desk, clad in her white suit.

I am making love to Phoebe. Her breathing has turned into a staccato moan. I open my eyes; I want to see her face in ecstasy, I want to be conscious that I am with her and not with the blondes.

As she calms down I become aware of her strong odor. It is not unpleasant but more pungent than the smell of blonde women, more erotic, more dizzying. The smell of blondes is sweeter, softer, more like a field of wheat. Phoebe's odor is threatening, demanding, and penetrating; it stays with you for days, everywhere: in the rooms, on the bed sheets, even on my hand.

We are lying next to one another, still out of breath. She reaches for my hand and turns her head toward me.

"What do couples do these days after a fuck if they don't smoke?" she asks dreamily.

"Eat," I say, and kiss her fingertips gently.

"What have you got in the fridge?"

"Nothing. I don't eat at home these days. Let's go out to dinner. I spend too much time in the apartment. I want to get out!" And I slap her ass hard in encouragement to move. She gets mad at me and wrestles playfully on the bed with me. Her sweaty, firm body feels wonderful. As we keep rolling back and forth I become conscious of having become old. Ten years ago, I would have had another erection by now.

I am quiet on our way to Café Roma. Phoebe is sensitive to my mood and doesn't say a word until we park and sit at a table on the terrace. It is unusually mild for a Los Angeles evening. Without the Santa Ana winds it would be too cool for dinner outside.

I am wondering if Dr. Atwill will show up tomorrow for lunch at the Bistro Garden. Her civilized manners and the natural curiosity of an educated person will drive her there—I am counting on it. Now that she is aware of my intention, and I am no longer her patient she might consider starting a relationship. You never know. An affair with her will definitely cure me of my obsession with Marika. Of course, there is the off chance that she might just come to put an end to my pursuit. It is easier to say no at a leisurely lunch than under the pressures and professional duties in her office.

There is a lot more to my fixation than a physical desire for blondes, the classic attraction between Jews and blonde Gentiles. Marika represents much more to me. She is responsible for confusing reality and unreality in my life.

From the age of eleven to sixteen she represented unreality for me because I believed she was unobtainable. In fact, she was real for me only I didn't recognize it and didn't take advantage of it at the time. Decades later she became unreal again, just an image in my fantasies.

For a long time I've been looking for a person who would breath life into her unreality, into a fantasy I have been harboring for forty years. And I have found that person in Dr. Atwill.

We ask for two "Cafe Roma" pizzas and a bottle of Valpolicella. This restaurant serves one of the best pizzas in town: thin, crunchy crust and only a moderate amount of dressing. It is not surprising that most of the tables are occupied all day long. I recognize some of the habitués: actors, well-known stars and producers with their portable phones placed on the table. Inside, a pianist belts out Italian kitsch–rather incongruous in Beverly Hills. On the other hand, Beverly Hills is a large market place for kitsch as well as for quality. Most people here would snub these songs but be ready to spend fortunes on a painting by Peter Max, believing it to be high art.

The waiter brings out the wine and asks me to taste it, interrupting our silence. I find it silly and embarrassing to go through these motions on a cheap bottle of Valpolicella. He fills our glasses and mutters something with such a heavy accent that I cannot understand. Phoebe nods in approval; she understood him. Being an immigrant, my hearing is attuned to North American accents; I tune out of any other heavily accented talk. I lift my glass.

"Good luck with your script!" I toast her. She smiles and clinks my glass.

"Anything happening with your projects?" she asks with genuine interest. The last thing I want to think about right now is work, movies and the art of cinema. I have spent nearly a lifetime making films and have made a number of serious mistakes, like everybody else. I listened too much to the advice of "*friends.*" I directed some films to practice my craft, others strictly to make money. Unfortunately, it is not that simple in the industry. Traditionally, the politics of art don't condone work you do for survival. If you don't have the means to sustain yourself you'll be forced to become a saint and live on water and air. You are expected to suffer for art. If you are fortunate enough to be born into a rich family you can redeem yourself by making films against your class and call it social consciousness. But if you want to do a film of lasting value, a story about the human condition, the nature of mankind, our soul, you'd better watch out, for the entire town will come down on you. The producers will tell you that you have a European sensibility and that Americans will not buy the stuff.

The more I think about these difficulties the more I realize that the heart of the problem lies with a few Philistine, greedy and superficial producers in the industry. Of course, I am guilty because I went along with them for a while and justified it to myself as an absolute necessity for survival. I was naive not to have foreseen the consequences. I wanted to work at any cost; I wasn't cut out for martyrdom. Selling out works for you only if the film makes a fortune at the box office; then, all is forgiven, despite the pans from critics.

"You're awfully quiet, Gabi," she mercifully interrupts my train of thought. "You haven't answered my question."

"I am not too optimistic about my feature projects these days. I'll probably do some TV work until my dream project is financed."

"Is that what's really bothering you, or is it something you don't want to talk about?" She sounds genuinely concerned.

"The older you get, the more problems you have to deal with. They accumulate like your birthdays."

"Don't get maudlin on me, Gabi. Just think about the real miseries people sustain in life. You've got it all. You shouldn't complain."

"You're right. I give the same advice to others."

Phoebe keeps taking glances at her watch as if she were late for a date.

"You need to be somewhere?" I ask innocently. Of course, I am not jealous at all. I know she goes out with younger guys; after all she is in school, bombarded by ceaseless temptations. I ask for the check and we leave.

Phoebe lives with her family on Lexington Road, a few blocks from the Beverly Hills Hotel above Sunset Boulevard. Her father is a well-respected showbiz attorney and her mother is a successful talent agent. Phoebe grew up in money and sophistication—not the ideal environment for fostering a realistic perspective on life. I presume her university education has helped her to develop, in most areas, a consciousness of basic human values.

I stop the car in her impressive driveway and, like a polite European man, step out to open the door on her side. As I walk around the car I notice a young man running toward us, dressed in black harem pants and a two-sizes-too-large leather jacket.

"Shit," I hear Phoebe's voice. We both reach the passenger seat at the same time.

"Where the fuck were you, bitch?" he yells at Phoebe, who doesn't move from her seat. "I've been waiting for two fucking hours cooped up in my goddamn car!" He looms over her with his hands on his hips. Then he looks at me with a moronic grin, collecting saliva in his mouth. I am standing next to him waiting and wondering if he will spit in my face or hers.

"And who the fuck is this guy, driving you all over town in a white fucking Porsche? Your professor of cinema?" He over emphasizes the word "professor," giving it a sarcastic edge. I look at Phoebe who is perfectly collected. She steps out of the car and looks at the young man disdainfully.

"Prick," she mumbles between her teeth, and strides toward the house wriggling her behind slightly more than she normally does. She enters without glancing back at us. The guy looks incredulously in her direction, then turns to me.

"Have you fucking ever seen a bitch like that before?" he asks rhetorically. He looks humiliated. "Rotten, spoiled little cunt. I'm going to kick her fucking ass tomorrow, the goddamn bitch." He turns and marches to his black Corvette, yanks the door open, hops in, starts the engine with a roar and peels away from the curb. Just then, a Beverly Hills police car turns the corner. The cops pull him over before he is in second gear. I get into my car and give him the thumbs-up sign as I drive by.

* * *

VI.

To me the world appeared orderly. Everybody and everything was in its right place and people looked and behaved comfortably in it. I viewed the world with detachment and indifference; I was self-centered and lacked empathy and compassion for others, except, perhaps, my immediate family members.

One day, toward the end of the summer in 1945, a few days before Hiroshima was destroyed by the first atomic bomb, we heard a loud, impatient banging on the door of our apartment and the ringing of the doorbell at the same time. Alarmed, my mother and I ran to the door. There was my brother, eleven years older than I, bald and skeletal, standing in the doorway, crying. We had given up on ever seeing him again. He was nineteen when the Hungarian Fascists took him to a forced labor camp, then later transferred him to an Austrian concentration camp in Mauthausen. My mother also burst into tears and threw her arms around him, kissing him. I was thrilled to see him alive.

For me, Steven had always been a perfect big brother. He defended me from street kids picking on me in a part of the city called *Chicago,* near where we lived. I wasn't much of a fighter but my brother used to beat up anti-Semite gang members on our street. He had his own gang, to my parents' chagrin, and was constantly getting into trouble with the authorities. It cost my father a fortune bribing the local police to drop charges.

He also took care of my education in matters of sex and the sartorial arts. He was a snazzy dresser and a few years after his return from the dead he became one of the best known playboys among the *Golden Youth* of Budapest. I wanted desperately to emulate him but I was too bookish and shy to follow smoothly in his footsteps.

My brother took after our father who was also a ladies' man. During my childhood, I witnessed a great many fights between my parents caused by my father's escapades. In Hungary, at that time, male chauvinism prevailed. As in France, men didn't divorce their wives and break up their families; they acquired mistresses instead. Even in a middle-class family, housewives were slaves. We didn't have any electrical kitchen appliances, a washing machine, vacuum cleaner or refrigerator in the apartment. My mother labored day and night for the three men in the family. After twenty years of this hard labor, she did not seem too desirable to my father. We all knew about his mistresses but once in a while my mother had to put up a fight to prove that she wasn't a fool.

Soon after my brother's return from Mauthausen, my father decided that I should learn to play a musical instrument. The main reason behind that decision wasn't his great concern for my education in classical music, though that was part of it. He secretly expected that I would learn his favorite Gypsy songs in no time and would accompany him and our guests—after a few drinks had loosened their tongues—in good Hungarian fashion.

On a Saturday morning, a black grand piano arrived unexpectedly. After some heated deliberation my mother and I found the perfect corner for it in our living room—a room hardly used except when guests came for dinner. In the wintertime we didn't go near the living room. There was no central heating system in the building and to heat up the large living room with coal took far too much time and trouble. Also, coal was scarce and expensive. So the family spent the winter days either in the kitchen or in the small, easily heated common room right next to it.

I loved our dinner parties. Soon after the liberation, my parents entertained some high-ranking Russian officers for dinner, who brought along bottles of vodka and drank and sang all night with my father. He was truly happy in those days. My father had become a local functionary on economic matters for the Communist Party. He was an excellent businessman and organizer. It was not until later, during the worst of the Stalin era, he became disillusioned with Communism.

My mother was a great cook who fulfilled her creative ambitions in the kitchen for those dinner parties. Her cooking and baking became the center of attention, for a few hours, at least. I always got sick eating too many of her fabulous cakes and pastries.

My full stomach would give me nightmares and erotic dreams about Marika. Ever since our memorable walk in the City Park I had tried to get up enough courage to ask her to play doctor, but never could. Right after seeing her, I would reconstruct our games at home and become infuriated at the memory of my cowardly behavior. I wanted to see her pussy badly, and was suffering physically from my curiosity.

These inner conflicts haunted my dreams. I knew one day I would ask her to satisfy my curiosity, but it had to be the right moment. Secretly, I was hoping she would offer it to me since she was the older of us.

The first female genitalia I finally saw—only a fleeting glance, nothing more—were not Marika's. Our street was close to one of the largest marketplaces in the city and in the summer, every second week, the market expanded into the neighboring streets. The merchants set up tent stalls on the sidewalks and traffic was blocked off. The streets came alive with noise and crowds of colorful people. I loved those days. The black market of the postwar period also integrated itself into the fair, its shady characters selling everything from American cigarettes to nylon stockings and phony wristwatches. I used to pass through the market twice a day on my way to school and back, stopping at the makeshift table of the guy who conned money out of gullible bystanders with *three card monte*. I played a few times until my brother explained what the guy was up to. A miserable way of making a living.

I enjoyed my walks through the crowd, rubbing against pretty young women and taking a peek at their boobs through the armpit slit of their summer dresses. Hungarian women didn't wear bras unless they badly needed a lift. Now that I had passed my twelfth birthday, my interests focused on Marika, science and the female body. I paid little attention to world and internal politics. I wanted to forget the war years.

One afternoon, as I ambled home from school through the fair, I noticed a group of Gypsy women parked on the sidewalk, holding onto their babies. Some stood, others sat and leaned against the wall of our building. They wore colorful, long skirts and loose blouses for easy access to their large boobs. Their dark, oily skin and bare feet looked dirty and unappealing–these women didn't embody the romantic ideal of the beautiful Gypsy. I didn't see any of their men nearby.

One of the women who sat against the wall was breast-feeding her baby. Just as I passed by with my eyes glued on her she yanked the baby's head from the breast and revealed a large nipple shooting in my direction. She shoved her huge breast back into the blouse–the biggest breasts I had ever seen–and pulled up her legs to place the baby on her knees. She was not wearing underwear. My heart started to pound so hard I could barely breathe. Finally, I saw it. A large, black mass of pubic hair with a pink, crumpled-looking vulva gaped at me. It wasn't what I expected; I didn't like the sight. But I was elated nonetheless. It was like losing your virginity and not quite knowing what happened. I hoped that I'd get to see Marika's and that it would look different. I knew instinctively that Marika's pubic area would be a lovely sight.

One day during the summer vacation–I must have been thirteen–I was practicing a popular hit song at the piano. I didn't notice Marika sneaking up behind me. My *bravura* performance so excited her that she gave me a big kiss, close to my lips. She had never kissed me there before. I wanted a lingering kiss, like the ones I saw in American movies, but she didn't know what I desired. Like most children, I believed if I wanted something really badly some one would read my mind and take the initiative, relieving me of all responsibilities.

I was still thinking about my inaction when she asked me with her innocent charm if I wanted to go with her to the Palatinus Baths. Of course I wanted to go; I would have gone to Bulgaria with her if she had asked. She already had a beach bag slung over her shoulder, packed and ready to go.

I wasn't a good swimmer and didn't like pools, but I liked watching the girls in bathing suits, particularly Marika.

Budapest is a city famous for its numerous springs, baths, and public pools. They are huge complexes of pools of various shapes and sizes, situated in the heart of the city at the most beautiful and picturesque spots. They are architectural splendors, some of them built in the 16th and 17th centuries. The most recent one, the Palatinus, was designed for the Olympic games. They all have restaurants and bars; people spend their weekends there. Going to a pool in Budapest is an all-day social activity. Cafe houses and swimming pools were the "in" places those days; they were the pick-up joints and centers for exhibitionism. This is why Hungarians are good at water sports, particularly at water polo.

Thank God Marika wasn't a good swimmer either.

When our bodies became too hot in the sun, she suggested we go into one of the shallow pools to cool off. Once in the water we inevitably started fooling around, splashing at each other, trying some breaststrokes and submerging ourselves. Once when I passed by her underwater I touched her thighs with my hands as if by accident. When we got tired of the game we sat at the shallow end of the pool where the fresh water poured in. Marika wore a one-piece swimsuit which showed off her long legs and budding boobs. I wished she were wearing a bikini.

After a while I ran out of acceptable pretexts for touching her leg. Everything that popped into my mind seemed too crude until I hit upon the most obvious excuse in the world.

One of the big attractions of this complex was a pool that generated waves at ten-minute intervals delighting those who had never been at sea. After considerable mental torment I mustered enough courage to suggest we try the wave pool. Marika thought it was a brilliant idea and even reproached herself for not having come up with it.

Holding hands, we plunged into the waves at the shallow end where we both felt safe. We floated together on the undulating water, hands squeezed in euphoric abandon, bumping each other's bodies playfully, intentionally, even hugging protectively once in a while to prevent the force of the waves separating us. Touching, squeezing, holding her wet body, feeling her smooth skin against my hands and legs fulfilled the day's promise. Those few minutes in the waves were my most exhilarating sexual experience yet.

We left the pool, still holding hands, and stretched out on the concrete steps to take in more sun. I watched her lying on her back with her legs pulled up. I couldn't stop gazing at her crotch, yearning to see under her bathing suit, hoping that by some miracle I would be able to without her being aware of it.

That night wild dreams tortured me again without mercy. Puberty was approaching, making my dreams erotic without yet being graphic. Soon, something happened that made me hopeful about Marika and our future.

One late summer day I was returning from school preoccupied with the idea of nuclear chain-reactions, a subject on everyone's mind since Hiroshima. A few days before I had read an article in a popular magazine on the subject and that morning asked my math teacher a lot of questions about it.

As I entered our building I was hoping to see Marika in her window waving at me. Instead, as I reached the courtyard I encountered a most bizarre and devastating sight. Marika's stepfather was stretched out on a long, wooden cart, completely naked, his skin looking like yellow wax. He was dead.

I ran upstairs, taking two and three steps at a time, and burst into the apartment out of breath. I asked my mother what happened to Mr. Toth. She told me without much fuss that he committed suicide by putting his head into the gas oven. When I asked why, she said nobody knew.

In a short while a black van came from the morgue and took him away. I watched from the living room window as two men in black uniforms loaded him in. The black morgue van was a terrifying sight for me throughout my childhood.

Weeks later I overheard my mother and aunt talking half in Hungarian and half in Yiddish about Mr. Toth's suicide. Whenever my parents spoke Yiddish in my presence the subject was always sexually oriented gossip. They didn't realize that at my age learning foreign languages was easy. It was amusing to me how naive they were. I understood enough words to figure out that Mr. Toth had molested Marika and his wife had found them *in flagrante delicto*. I've never found out how far he went. After this event I didn't see Marika for a long while.

Then, one day, my mother broke the news during lunch that the Toths were moving upstairs into the small apartment next to ours. I was delighted but didn't show it. I kept on eating and talking about school and my chemical experiments. As I was trying to squeeze some money out of my mother for some lab equipment, I noticed Marika's mother outside our window, carrying boxes. The window of our little room opened onto the corridor of the court-yard. Those old buildings were constructed in such a way that the corridors were in the open air circling inside the large courtyard, protected by a cast iron railing. Thus, everyone's activities were constantly on display; one couldn't escape scrutiny. Soon after her mother passed by our window Marika came along with small pieces of furniture.

My mother wasn't a bit happy about this move, but she didn't let on.

* * *

VII.

I ARRIVE AT The Bistro Garden five minutes to one o'clock. An obsequious Maitre d' grinningly leads me to my table in the "garden," a simple tent furnished with cast iron tables and remarkably uncomfortable chairs. I ask the hovering waiter for a bottle of mineral water and see the beam on his face melt into a reluctant grimace.

I had picked the Bistro Garden for purely strategic reasons. I wanted to propose a restaurant so well known that Dr. Atwill couldn't forget it or pretend to forget it. Had I hung around explaining the whereabouts of a small, romantic restaurant she would have had the time to turn me down.

The Bistro Garden is a landmark restaurant in Beverly Hills, and is vastly overrated. From the outside it looks like any of the thousands of square, pink stucco buildings put together in a hurry to disgrace the lower skyline of the city. The inside is decorated in 19th century imitation French bistro style. The designers must have presumed that elegance, good taste and lots of money go hand in hand, and together they ensure quality food. Unfortunately, that presumption in this case proves false. The place does project, however, a certain aura of ersatz European opulence; it is a pretentious reminder to local patrons that the old world lifestyle can be lived here just as well as in Paris.

I am sure she won't stand me up. I am more concerned about the outcome of this lunch. This relationship, if I may call it that, has started off on an awkward note. I was too convincing at pretending I wasn't romantically interested; it will be difficult to reverse her attitude now, even though she knows what I am after. Why do I keep fooling myself?

Dr. Atwill arrives ten minutes late. She wears a white suit—not the same one she wore the first time I saw her on Wilshire Boulevard—and smells like a salesgirl at Chanel. Since she didn't wear perfume in her office at our sessions I am wondering if it is a good sign, or completely meaningless. Because it is immensely hot outside she could be concerned about body odor. On the other hand, if she believes that the natural smell of the body is more stimulating than artificial scents, she could be trying to temper my interest.

I rise from my seat to shake her hand and slip the chair politely under her perfect buttocks like a well brought-up man. I detect a suppression of a smile, as if to persuade me that her decision to lunch with me is nothing more than a professional gesture, and that she will have to put an end to this business during our forthcoming conversation. As these thoughts zip through my mind the waiter bounces over to our table like Baryshnikov would approach the dying swan.

"A Chivas on the rocks, please," she announces without thinking. Is she a heavy drinker I am wondering? Perhaps she is nervous about meeting me. That is a good sign. Before I have a chance to welcome her with a few well-chosen words, she attacks me.

"I am very angry at you." She overemphasizes the word "very" as if she were reprimanding a naughty child.

"Oh?" I say instinctively, ready to add, Then why did you come to lunch with me? But I change my mind; I don't want to alienate her on our first date. "Let's take a look at the menu first, shall we?"

She looks at me with darts in her eyes, then buries her head in the giant menu. The more pretentious a restaurant the larger the size of the menu, it seems.

Too preoccupied with the unfolding situation I am unable to concentrate on the choice of food. While I am trying to read the menu the waiter recites the specials with the speed of a Yeshiva student reading the Torah. I close the menu and listen to the litany, and keep my eyes on her at the same time. She seems collected and attentive. After some serious deliberation she decides on a veal dish. I order the fish of the day with a sigh of relief. That's out of the way. I didn't come here to enjoy my food, I came here to seduce Cass Atwill. On the other hand, if I decide to enjoy my meal, perhaps I will get further with my seduction. Who can tell?

I notice the waiter has left the wine list on our table. As I pick it up my eyes stay on her face. Our eyes meet. Her expression is soft now, but inscrutable. I smile at her without provocation; it is a friendly smile to suggest peace.

"Would you like some wine with your meal?" I ask as gently as I can. I don't want to rupture her Scotch-induced mood.

"Why don't you order a bottle of Montrachet," she asks as if it were the most natural thing to order in California. I don't remember ever having seen Montrachet on a Los Angeles wine list. She has probably decided to give me a hard time, or has just returned from Paris and is still in the habit of ordering from Lasserre's wine list.

"I don't see Montrachet on this wine list," I mumble, while trying to find something she won't reject.

"Why don't we try a bottle of local Chardonnay?" she says. "You can't go wrong with that." I agree and make a half-hearted attempt to catch the eye of the wine waiter. As I turn my head, I nod to a few superficial acquaintances nearby. What if my neck gets stuck and my head can't turn back? How embarrassing even to think about it, to be stuck with my head twisted and frozen like a marionette.

In the meantime she finishes her scotch and leans back on her chair revealing a little more cleavage than she showed at the office. I realize she is not wearing a blouse under her suit jacket. Does she want to seduce me? It cannot be. I think she is just teasing me. Most shrinks suffer serious mental or psychological disorders, I am told. The shrinks I knew back in Montreal (friends of course), were all crazies.

At last, I catch the waiter's attention. He sprints over to our table and I give the order. I look at Dr. Atwill again, wondering if I can make my first move, if everything else is out of the way.

"Do you spend most of your life with these people?" she asks condescendingly as she scans the crowd.

"I wouldn't go that far," I say defensively. "I am more discriminating, and I don't come here often. I thought you might like it here. Don't you?" I realize she has confused me again and I no longer know what I am talking about. "More discriminating", what is this? I must maintain control during lunch otherwise she is going take over and that will be the end of the relationship.

"Well, I can do without these pretentious places. I prefer, to borrow your classification of the world, reality to unreality."

"Would you rather go to another restaurant?" I ask without meaning it. I don't think I could handle another round of ordering drinks and food.

"No, no. I'll manage to live through this. Don't be offended by my comments." She says without meaning it, too.

The food arrives unbelievably fast. It must have been ready made and shoved into the microwave oven at the last minute. It is a food factory here, not a restaurant. We taste our food but don't comment on it. I take a sip of the wine and nod to the waiter to pour it. I am thinking of a toast as the waiter leaves but she beats me to it.

"To your fast recovery!" she says loudly, and with a touch of self-congratulation for finding a way to be sarcastic.

"It's up to you," I say, and look into her eyes longingly. She laughs out loud, like she did once in her office.

"I am not a follower of the Masters and Johnson school of sex therapy, you must understand that, Gabi." She used my first name. Does it mean anything? Not necessarily in America, particularly in Los Angeles. In her office she kept calling me Mr. Fodor. Well, we are in a restaurant; she is just being polite.

For a while we both eat in silence. I am becoming more and more aware of the irresistible erotic effect she has on me. Must be the combination of her physical beauty, her intelligence, the heavy, provocative perfume, the teasing view of her cleavage, and the face—Marika's face. I am mesmerized by her presence. I have to make love to her; I can't let this once-in-a-lifetime opportunity slip by. But am I making the old mistake again? Am I pursuing unreality? I should walk out on her right now before it is too late.

"You're quiet, suddenly. Is there something wrong?" Her question interrupts my self-torturing. Shall I answer her honestly? I can't. I must play the game. Seduction is an intricate, often dangerous game. Just think about the vicissitudes recorded in Casanova's diary.

"Are you married, Cass?" I casually ask using her first name. She gave me the permission to do so by using mine.

"What difference does it make? You must understand, Gabi, this lunch is not a date. I did you a favor showing up. I didn't want to humiliate you by standing you up in front of your distinguished colleagues here. You're wasting your time and energy, you're pursuing an unrealistic dream. Why don't you realize its absurdity?"

"I don't see it as unrealistic and absurd at all. You're a woman and I'm a man. What's absurd about an affair between two consenting adults? My initial approach may not have been subtle or conventional . . . " She laughs again heartily.

"What if I told you that I'm not interested in you—as a man. I don't have to like you because you wish it or make me part of your fantasy life."

"Perhaps you're too much of a bourgeois, Cass."

"Now you're putting labels on me," she interrupts. "You know what, Gabi? I think, deep down, you are a bourgeois, and perhaps that's the root of your problem. You consider yourself a free person, an artist . . . because you're doing artistic work. But working in the arts doesn't necessarily make you an artist. Why don't you examine yourself first before calling people bourgeois?"

She has touched a nerve. Maybe she is right and I am still a bourgeois with strong middle-class habits. So what? Art is classless. True, universal art cuts through class boundaries; it doesn't discriminate. But have I done such work yet? I will not judge myself at the moment. I must separate my emotional problems from my creative ones. But can I? They go hand in hand. One helps the other to survive; they nourish each other.

I am eating in silence and thinking of a new tack. I don't want to argue the same point over again. She was right; I had no right to call her a bourgeois, it was not in good taste.

"Don't you find it stimulating when a man honestly tells you the effect you have on him?"

"No, I don't. I much prefer a subtle game of seduction. Actually, I must correct myself. I'd prefer it if I were interested in being seduced at all."

"One cannot be interested in being seduced. Seduction is an act that runs up against resistance. If you are interested at all it's not seduction anymore; it's simply succumbing to a conventional courting game. What makes seduction exciting is the gradual breakdown of resistance on the part of the one who's being seduced." She has been concentrating fiercely on her veal cutlet during my lecture without glancing in my direction. I don't think she likes my argument. I think I have insulted her.

"Regardless of strategy, I'm not game for an affair, and that's the bottom line," she declares, and gently wipes her mouth with the damask napkin.

"I see," I mutter between bites of the dreadful fish I ordered. The nerve cells in my nose are tormented by the smell. The fish must have begun to decompose before it was broiled. The morgue must smell like this. I wonder if I will smell the same or worse, when the time comes. Is anyone I love going to smell my decomposing flesh? Probably not. I will be buried by then, unless I die under special circumstances, such as in a plane crash or an earthquake, or from some new horrible disease. But why am I thinking about death? These days I think as much about death as about love and sex.

As we walk out of the restaurant she leads the way. I try to guess what sort of car she drives. Probably a BMW or a Saab. We both give our tickets to the valet and wait. Neither of us speaks. I don't feel like starting some small talk and she doesn't initiate any either. So we stand silently there in the unbearable heat. I notice that my armpit is wet. I don't think it is from the heat; it is more like anxiety sweat, which smells immediately once it's been secreted.

Her car arrives. It is a navy blue BMW. A shrink in Beverly Hills who helps showbiz people cope with success and failure. An elegant woman, she must make a fortune. The exploiters of troubled psyches. Are they more ethical than those hard-nosed businessmen exploiting the working class? Probably not. They have a humanistic excuse though: the Hippocratic oath.

"Thanks for the lunch, Gabi." She steps toward her car and turns to me. "And forget Marika's face. Find yourself a young starlet and make her a superstar.

The process will help you forget. And when she leaves you for the leading man, come see me again. Perhaps, I'll be able to help you." Just before she steps into her car she smiles at me with pity. "Bye, now," she says. Her BMW pulls away with a hiss.

Rejection is the course of the day in Hollywood. One must develop a thick skin to survive. Hundreds of scripts are submitted daily to studios, thousands of producers, writers and directors compete for the few that are made into films. It is miraculous when a project becomes a movie. I don't take rejection personally but most people do. After years of humiliation I have become fairly immune but maybe those turndowns accumulate in your psyche and eventually I will end up on Dr. Atwill's couch. Or, I will make my masterpiece, get an Oscar, be saved by the grace of God and live safely for a few years until I make another turkey. There is no end to the vicious circle.

I start up my car and drive aimlessly for a while. Then I decide to get a haircut in the Century City shopping mall. After, I may drop in to Brentano's to check out the new books. As I am driving west on Santa Monica Boulevard Phoebe's image pops into my mind. It is too early to call her. Also, I don't want to give her the impression that I am after her. I may call her this evening for dinner so I won't have to eat by myself.

The experience with Cass at lunch has left me with an unpleasant after-taste. Despite her attitude toward me I still want to make love to her. She could be playing hard-to-get—who can tell? I am not sure I like her as a person yet, but I want to fuck her at least once and watch her face. I imagine the experience will be enough for me to forget Marika for the rest of my life. I need just one experience. The question is, how am I going to go about it? She won't answer my calls, I am sure of that. She probably walks to work every day, like the other day when I first saw her on Wilshire Boulevard. On that particular day she could have had her car in the shop and decided to walk instead of take a cab, which means that she lives nearby. Her husband would have driven her to work if she were married. She most likely walks to work every day. Well, tomorrow morning I will wait for her near the medical building and find out. But what am I going to tell her that I haven't already said? I must think about it more.

Instead of having a haircut I decide to go home and sit at the poolside with a book. I hang a left at Century Park East and drive to my apartment building and down to the garage. It is too hot to leave the car in the courtyard.

There is a message on my answering machine from Phoebe that I should call as soon as I get in. It is unlike her to leave urgent messages for me. The number is unfamiliar to me, probably it is her boyfriend's. I dial and she picks it up instantly. Her voice is a little faded and weak but recognizable.

"Guess where I am," she asks. I can see her characteristic grin in my mind.

"You sound as if you're in bed with your boyfriend."

"I am in bed, all right. In a hospital bed."

"Did you have an abortion?" I ask, and regret it instantly. "Sorry, I was just kidding. What happened to you?"

"Come and visit me and I'll tell you all about it. Cedars Sinai, Room 4039."

Seeing friends or relatives in hospitals is not my favorite pastime. I dread the idea of being hospitalized and can't help thinking about it when I am in one. Hospitals are the anterooms to the grave. My mother used to spend a lot of time in hospitals and she loved it. For her, it was a holiday, a chance to be away from us and the all-day grind at home.

I take a shower to wash off the malodorous memories of my lunch with Cass. Why does she wear white all the time? What does she hide under that conventual habit? She must be rotten to the core—no heart or soul left to sustain humanity in that perfect body. I start to think crazy notions about her. I must stop. I must not take her rejection too seriously. But how can I take it lightly when I have spent decades waiting for this moment? I can't write it off or forget it overnight. I must seduce her at any cost. Perhaps I should kidnap her and force her to spend a weekend with me. But it is stupid; she would have me locked up in no time.

Maybe fucking Cass wouldn't erase my recurring fantasies about Marika. Maybe a substitute wouldn't work. Can we really fool our minds? Why can't I leave my past alone, forget about the unfulfilled childhood dreams and live for the present or the future?

There is an unfathomable engine inside me driving this obsessive behavior. It is my unreality syndrome again. Reality doesn't stimulate me, only the unattainable realm of unreality, the intangible reflection in the mirror. Is this the reason I became a film director? I never thought about it that way before though it should have occurred to me. Yes, that's it. I am creating dreams on the screen, a world of unreality, visions of an obsessed mind. What do those visions reveal about existence? Have I ever made anything revelatory on the screen—images, ideas which penetrate deeply enough to reflect truth (near truth would be enough) rather than unreality? How do we find truth in a reflected image? Perhaps we must distort it just enough to draw attention to the truth. If you are not careful you overdo it and it becomes unreality again—a grotesque one. It is a delicate operation; you need a surgeon's hand to twist the mirror just so. Then, truth ultimately will face you. But you have to work fast too, otherwise your hand will start shaking and you will lose the grip on the mirror. You will lose the revelation.

I stand in front of the door to Phoebe's private room in Cedars Sinai Hospital with a dozen white daisies in my hand, wondering what sort of sight is in store for me. I am certain it won't be the same as the surprises she often pulls on me in my bedroom. Hospitals are not conducive to sexual fantasies, as far as I am concerned; but the world is made up of different temperaments. I must stop being infantile—self-centered about the world.

I gently knock on the door and enter. There is this automatic, instinctive reverence toward invalids. One of those silly things we were brought up on. I should have banged on the door and barged in. I am sure she is fine.

She is on the bed bolt upright reading a book. I don't get to see the title right away because my eyes are drawn to her nose and eyes. The first thing that crosses my mind is that she was in an accident. Her nose and both eyes are black and yellow with a touch of poison green mixed in.

"Did you have a nose job?" I say kiddingly but actually mean it. Why didn't I think about it immediately? But she wouldn't be in Cedars Sinai for a nose job. So, I change my expression and pretend to be empathetic.

"Yes, I did have a nose job," she says bitterly. "That motherfucker boyfriend of mine gave it to me. Next day, after that incident in front of our house, he waited for me at the lecture hall and broke my nose. Can you believe it? The little fuck."

"Yes, I can believe it. You should be more discriminating . . . "

"Don't lecture me today, Gabi. Just sit on the bed and hold my hand." I take the book out of her hand—it is Eisenstein's *Film Form and Film Sense*—and put it on the bedside table that is crowded with flowers, probably from her parents.

"Tell me more about it—if you want to," I say, affecting grave concern.

"There is not much more to tell you other than I decided to have my nose fixed at the same time. They'll have to operate on me anyway so I instructed them to throw in a nose job. Wasn't it clever? I always wanted one anyway."

"It sure was," I mumble without enthusiasm. "There is nothing wrong with your nose. It's beautiful."

"It's too Jewish," she says with a slight grimace.

"But you are Jewish. What's wrong with a Jewish nose? Look at mine!" I declare proudly and show her my profile, hoping she'll say I don't have a Jewish nose.

"You're a guy. You don't want to run around with Sissy Spacek's nose, do you?"

"What if you hate the job they do?"

"I'll break the shithead's nose and put him through the same fucking miseries I went through."

"You should sue the little punk."

"Don't you worry, my father is on his case. He says the jerk will stand trial for this."

"Do you have any witnesses?" I ask innocently.

"No, I don't. You've got to be my witness, Gabi. He was smart to hit me with nobody around." She acts as if perjury were the most natural thing in the world.

"Me? But I wasn't even around when it happened," I say in protestation.

"So what?"

"I am not going to commit perjury, not even for you. It's a felony, don't you know? How could you presume I'd do such a thing? Don't they teach you ethics in college these days?" I am getting seriously angry at her nonchalance.

"Don't get carried away with your moralizing, Gabi. It was just an idea. You're right, let's drop it."

But before I can relax, she continues. "You could do one thing, though." Oh, God! What now?

"Will you tell the judge what happened the night before? How he abused me in front of you, and so on?"

"You can count on that. I'll tell him the truth. That's all right with me."

She tries to smile at me but it hurts.

"You still have an opportunity to change your mind on the nose job."

"My father is against it, too."

"What about your mother?"

"My mother? Are you kidding? She should have married a plastic surgeon. She practically lives with one. He's working her over every six months from head to toe."

"Well, I like the way you are, if it means anything to you."

"Of course it does." She scans the room with glittering eyes—what happened to her suddenly?—and stops on the door.

"Gabi," she breathes in a tone that instantly alarms me. "Would you check that door, please. See if you can lock it?"

"You can't lock hospital room doors, Phoebe," I protest, knowing perfectly well what she is up to. "Why do you want it locked, anyway?"

"Can't you guess?" Her eyes twinkle.

"No, I can't guess," I lie, with a touch of annoyance.

"I get horny lying in bed all day. I want a quickie. It'll relax me . . . "

"But, Phoebe!" I yell incredulously, "you're in a hospital, you're supposed to suffer . . . "

"Don't be so goddamn conventional," she snaps, then pouts like a little girl who has just been told by her mother not to touch herself. "Give me your hand!"

I let her take my hand. With a quick move that prevents any resistance from me, she shoves my hand under the blanket and up to her crotch. I don't want to disappoint her so I begin slowly to masturbate her while keeping an eye on the door. She closes her eyes.

I see in my mind Cass's face be transformed into Marika's and take on that exalted expression that I have never seen but dreamt of for years in painful daydreams and wet night dreams—all unfulfilled and meaningless, wasted in fantasy land, in unreality.

* * *

VIII.

I DIDN'T LIKE myself much in my early teens. I was shy and a weakling. The sports I participated in, soccer and basketball, I played halfheartedly and irregularly, so I didn't develop muscle on my small bone structure. Nobody inspired me to change my body; I believed it was my destiny that clothes would fit me as if I was a wire hanger. I didn't look good in a bathing suit and was envious of kids who were muscular and strongly built, but I didn't do anything about it until the age of twenty-two when I emigrated to Canada. I wanted to get rid of my past completely, including my natural build.

I tried hard to overcome my strong sense of physical inferiority by reading more and more—anything I could put my hands on. Also, I avoided confrontations with bullies in school. Though I often went to the public pools, I always felt uncomfortable revealing my slight build for fear of looking ridiculous. My parents, my brother, my friends and relatives constantly nagged me to eat more and participate in sports.

Such encouragements didn't help my self-image. I retreated to my little corner in our common room (I didn't have a room of my own) and browsed the encyclopedia, my favorite reading at the time, and some Hungarian classics.

Very soon I got tired of reading Hungarian authors; I wanted to know about the world outside of Hungary. I became more interested in reading French and English novels but we didn't have many books at home and the school libraries were limited in foreign fiction. A year or so later I discovered the public libraries and began reading Dickens, Hugo and Verne aside from my readings in science.

Later, one winter weekend, I think I was about sixteen years old, snow blanketed overnight the mountains of Buda, the left bank of Budapest, to the delights of those who owned ski equipment. In those days skiing was a luxury and a highly desirable sport for the golden youth of Budapest and, of course, my brother owned a pair of skis. I had never been on skis before and thought it would be glamorous to glide down the mountain, watching the beautiful women in stylish ski suits. And, one never knew, I might get lucky if I kept my eyes open and tried hard to meet a girl with blond hair dancing in the wind as she descended the mountain. It didn't occur to me that I hadn't received any instructions and that I've never been on skies before. I thought arrogantly that I could just pick it up as I went along; skiing seemed easy when I watched others doing it.

My brother didn't object to lending me his equipment but warned me to be careful and try only the gentle slopes. I managed somehow to put together an outfit that didn't look too ridiculous. The boots I wore were not made for skiing but I had no choice; my brother's boots were too large.

None of my friends skied so I went alone. It was a cool sunny day and I was excited by the promise of adventure and felt privileged to carry the heavy skies on my narrow shoulder as I walked to the nearby streetcar stop. I was hoping to bump into Marika and her new boyfriend on the staircase, showing off, but it didn't happen.

Those days in the mountains of Buda there was no such thing as a ski lift. One had to carry the skis up the hill after each run and by the end of the day I had worked up a real appetite. I was careful at the first couple of runs on an easy slope and watched closely some good skiers to figure out their technique. It was naive of me to believe that I could learn to ski by osmosis but in those days I felt I could do anything I put my mind to without learning about it seriously.

Soon, I was sweating from the long hikes back to the top of the mountain and my legs began to shake. I stopped and watched with envy the guys and girls who skied with style unlike me doing the "snow-plow" all the way down the hill.

On my sixth run it happened. It had to happen. My legs gave in and my skis crossed in front throwing me into a snow bank. There were no safety bindings those days and my ankle twisted with the ski on my left foot, spraining it seriously. I managed to limp home but the next day my ankle had swollen badly and I couldn't step on that foot. I was bed-ridden for weeks and refused to see a doctor for fear that he would put my foot in a cast.

With nothing better to do, I read all day. A friend from school who was good at literature brought me a Balzac novel, "The Lost Illusions," and my life was changed overnight. I began reading serious books, mostly French literature, without taking a break. I was hooked. After I returned to school I started going to art galleries and began dabbling in painting. By the next year, my interests in science had faded and I developed a strong passion for all the arts.

It was a natural progression for me to move from a general interest in the arts, to a passion for watching movies, to making films. Film comprises all the art forms and being a director one makes use of the arts in every phase of the filmmaking process. In Hungary, film directing has been a highly regarded profession and my parents were happy that I chose it as my life's ambition.

In 1947, before the Communist Party came to power, the Boy Scouts existed in Hungary, in keeping with the country's Anglophile sentiments. My parents and my brother urged me to join in the hope that the weekend hikes in the mountains of Buda would strengthen me physically. So I decided to join them, as did my good friend Irvin, who contrary to me, needed to trim his bulging torso.

Hating regimentation and the taking of orders from some make-believe authority, I was uncomfortable with the military aspect of the Scouts. However, like most kids, girls, and infantile men, I was seduced by a uniform. I secretly hoped that it would help me succeed with Marika. I rushed out to buy my uniform and spent long moments in front of the mirror adjusting my scarf and trying to find the perfect angle for my hat.

According to their rules, Scouts didn't wear their uniforms indiscriminately but only on hikes, at meetings and in parades. I, however, put mine on every day after school and stood in the corridor in front of our kitchen door, leaning over the railing, as if in deep thought about the world, waiting for Marika to show up. One day she did. She stopped in front of me, looked me over and planted a quick kiss on my cheek. "You look cute," she said, and invited me to listen to some new jazz records she had just bought.

Delighted by my success, I followed her into her apartment that was just a kitchen and a room which served as both bedroom and sitting room for her and her mother. It wasn't much of a place but they couldn't afford anything better. At that time there was a serious housing shortage in Hungary. Even during the Fifties, just before the Revolution, finding an apartment was a problem for newlyweds.

The Toths didn't even have a bathroom in their apartment. They washed in the kitchen and used a common toilet in the corridor that served a few other small apartments as well.

Unfortunately, Mrs. Toth was at home and my hopes of being alone with Marika and playing some innocent games that might lead to something sexual were quickly derailed. Mrs. Toth also liked my Boy Scout uniform and pressed me tightly to her chest with a seductive smile. I could smell her unwashed dark skin but I didn't mind; in fact, I enjoyed it. She offered me some coffee.

As Mrs. Toth fluttered about in the kitchen making the coffee, her gown came loose, showing her short slip underneath and part of her breasts. She didn't pay any attention. I sensed that she knew she wasn't decent but deliberately didn't do anything about it, that she was playing games with me. She was a flirt and I suspected all along that she was the mistress of her boss, a middle-aged man who owned a shoe factory right across from us.

Marika was in the bedroom changing. As I stood in the middle of the kitchen stealing quick glances at Mrs. Toth's partial nudity, I felt I was cheating on Marika. I was halfway through my café-au-lait when she came out of the bedroom also wearing a gown. It was a wrap-around style that kept gaping open in front whenever she made a swift move.

She pulled me excitedly into the bedroom-cum-living-room to listen to her new Duke Ellington record. A strong female smell still lingered in the air, mixed with a heavy dose of carbon dioxide. I was going to suggest that she open the window but when she began to dance solo to the gentle rhythm of the music I decided to let the mood develop uninterrupted. She seemed about to do a striptease for me but then suddenly she grabbed my hands and pulled me to the center of the room. I didn't know how to dance. I knew about some dance schools in Budapest but always considered myself too young to enroll. Marika didn't mind my awkwardness at all; in fact, she was amused by it and enjoyed showing me some simple steps. I wondered where she learned to dance so well. The thought made me feel jealous but I refused to ask questions.

I was physically and emotionally intoxicated by holding on to her hand and waist, by stealing glances at her bare thigh under the loose gown that became looser as our dance steps became more frenetic. Once or twice I got a glimpse of her white panties. By the time the number was over I had my first hard-on. It was wonderful, but painful. The memory of that sweeping masculine pride still remains with me.

I wasn't sure what to do next: to keep on dancing, to draw Marika closer to me (I was too shy to do that), or sit for a while. My eyes lost focus by the time the number ended. We had stopped moving. I kept holding on to her for a while until Mrs. Toth entered the room asking Marika to play one of her favorite hit songs, "Chattanooga Choo-choo" translated into Hungarian.

While Marika searched for the song, I turned away from them for fear of revealing the tumescence in my short pants. I sat dreamily on their unmade bed wondering whose nightgown was casually thrown over the pillows. The sight of the pink silk nightie increased my torment. A sharp pain in my groin, never before experienced, alarmed me and doubled me up, though I understood instinctively that it must be the price I had to pay for the pleasures awaiting me in the future.

I felt dizzy. I knew I was far too young for the big event. I kept wondering how I would be able to endure this same pain every time I saw Marika. She saw that something was wrong with me and came over to sit next to me on the bed. Without any lewd intention, she put her hand on my bare leg and asked about my sudden change of mood. Her touch increased my pain sharply. I told her I was feeling funny and that I should go home. I stood and left in a hurry. My erection was gone by the time I entered our apartment but the pain persisted for a good while. Everything I thought about, everything I saw around me seemed to trigger fantasy images of Marika and her stepmother.

I kept wondering if girls were aware of the pains and sufferings they caused young boys who came within the vicinity of their blossoming sexuality.

Until the liberation, I lived in constant fear of death. Nothing but survival was on my mind. Now, it was sex and girls that gave me pain and misery. Sex and death, the two most powerful forces of nature tormented me from childhood.

I ran straight into the living room and began to pound the piano. I needed the distraction, the relief from frustration. I kept thinking about how my brother would have seduced Marika by now. He wasn't interested in young girls; he dated the most beautiful women in Budapest. But I knew he would have handled Marika and her mother differently.

My brother often asked me jokingly if I had fucked Marika yet. I usually blushed and said, "Not yet, but I will, soon." He remarked casually that, "She probably fucked like a rabbit—anyone could get into her pants." I hated listening to those comments about the girl I loved. I didn't really believe what he said; I considered it part of his customary bravado and general notions about women. I think he believed most women were sluts.

For a long while I tried to figure out ways to attract Marika to me, to force her to make the first move. At a general meeting of the Boy Scouts I saw some kids wearing white, navy officer's hats which looked elegant and sexy. They were Marine Scouts. I quickly concluded that if I wore a hat like that with my uniform Marika would instantly be attracted to me—if she had any sense at all.

I approached their patrol leader, a good-looking eighteen year old, pompous and arrogant, and told him I wanted to join the Marine Scouts. He looked me over with disgust and disbelief on his face, and sneered, "Come back when you're sixteen."

Years later I ran into him in Montreal. He had not changed much, but I had. We became quite good friends during my sojourn in Canada, but I never forgave him for rejecting me for the Marine Scouts.

One hot summer day, as I lugged blocks of ice in a pail from a vendor a few blocks down our street for our primitive ice box, a job my mother asked me to do every day in the summer, I came upon an inspired idea.

At noon, when the temperature rose to its highest, I went over to Marika's and casually told her she was welcome to take showers in our bathroom whenever she wanted to during those really hot days. She was enthusiastic about my invitation and said she would take me up on the offer one day. She had just washed herself down in her kitchen a few minutes before.

Since my mother was a prisoner of her household duties, she hardly spent time out of the apartment except in the morning at the marketplace. She spent hours there bargaining with the farmers. I hoped if Marika came over at all for her cold shower it would be in the morning when my mother was out. Though I couldn't decide how to handle myself while she was taking the shower, I fantasized that I would barge into the bathroom and watch her in the nude as she stood under the stream of water. I had no idea what she would do when I walked in—scream, smile, invite me to join her in the tub? It was all speculation, stimulating and frustrating.

During the summer vacation, I stayed at home on weekday mornings experimenting with chemicals. At the time, way before my ski accident, I wanted to be a research chemist and so I stank up the apartment every day with foul smelling salts.

I was in the process of making a solution of some cobalt salt in a retort and was just about to add a few drops of sulfuric acid when I heard a knock on the kitchen door. Annoyed by the interruption, I rushed out of our common room to open the door. Marika was standing there in her familiar gown with a towel thrown over her shoulder. I let her in without saying a word. I didn't know whether I should first shut off my Bunsen burner or welcome her with some clever "double entendre." She said she would love to take a quick shower before going to her dance class in the afternoon. I immediately thought of my brother's remark about her. She is probably seeing a boyfriend before the class to make love, that is the reason she wants to take a shower now. I quickly wiped the thought out of my mind, turned off the burner under the retort and with trembling legs led Marika into the bathroom. She thanked me and closed the door behind her.

My entire body shaking, I stayed in the hallway and listened to the noises from the bathroom. It was quiet for a while. I knew she was taking off her wrap-around gown and stepping out of her panties, or she could have come over without wearing them. I would have given ten years of my life if she had let me roll down her panties for her.

I had to sit down. What am I going to do next? I kept thinking. I couldn't get up enough courage to barge in and attempt to make love to her. I wouldn't have known where to start.

Then, I heard the shower starting up and her little gasps as the cold water knocked the air out of her lungs. I tried to picture her as she picked up the soap and began rubbing it over her body. Here was a mental torture I had never experienced before. Would I ever find any relief? Or, would I go through every day in misery until I was old enough to marry? I had no other choice but to walk in and surprise her. What would she do if I did that? I would never find out if I didn't try. But I couldn't get up from my chair. As I sat there glued to the seat, my groin throbbing and aching, my eyes fell upon the door to the water closet. In those days in Hungary there was no toilet in the bathroom. We had a separate room for that purpose. I knew immediately what to do.

Both the bathroom and the water closet contained windows onto a square shaped airshaft. The bathroom window happened to be right behind the bathtub, and the window in the water closet was situated above the toilet bowl. On tiptoe I rushed to the water closet, quietly opened the door, climbed up on the toilet cover and faced a perfect view.

How wonderful it was! Marika stood in the tub with her back to me exhibiting the most exquisite buttocks imaginable. My pulse raced. This was my first view of a naked female body; she was a perfectly proportioned creature. I was seeing a mermaid from a fairy tale. She never turned around but I didn't mind; this was enough excitement for one day. In a few minutes the mirage vanished. I left the water closet and went back to our common room to attend to my chemicals.

I didn't have to wait long before she came into the room, her long blonde hair dripping with water, and thanked me for the shower. I pretended to be busy with my experiment to avoid her gaze for fear of divulging my secret. With her cooled off and still wet lips, she planted a quick kiss on my cheek.

As soon as she left the apartment I packed away my chemistry set and ran over to my friend Irvin's, to give him a detailed account of the event. I had to tell someone and he was my best friend and confidant.

Irvin lived with his parents in a two-room apartment with a kitchen. A widow and her two teenage daughters occupied one of the rooms. The only way to reach Irvin's room was to walk through her quarters; there was no hallway separating the rooms. Such were the living conditions in Budapest right after the war.

On entering the widow's room from the small kitchen, I caught a glimpse of one of the girls as she was pulling a dress over her head. She was standing there in her pink panties without a bra, her gorgeously shaped boobs protruding. She didn't see me cross the room.

By the time I sat down in Irvin's room I was shaking again. It was too much for a thirteen-year-old boy to endure in one day. Irvin's parents were out so we could talk freely. He told me that those girls were always in a state of dressing or undressing and that he was used to it by now. I told him about my experience with Marika and the pains I had in my groin, but he didn't recognize the sensation. Then, I remembered that Irvin suffered some problems with his thyroid glands and was getting hormone treatments every week. He obviously wasn't turned on by those girls next door as badly as I was by Marika.

Irvin was rather stoical about my story. He couldn't have really known how I felt about Marika and girls in general. In theory he agreed that one day we were going to get laid, but he wasn't in any great hurry. He didn't want to go out of his way to manipulate girls into submission as I did.

I was in a rage. I didn't know what to do with myself, how to remove those images from my mind. I didn't realize then that one never rids oneself of images of past experiences; instead they get neatly packed away in the subconscious where they can torment a person for the rest of his life.

Ever since my rejection by the Marine Scouts, I had searched for ways to increase my status with the Boy Scouts. Without much difficulty I persuaded my father to buy me a bugle. I figured if I learned to blow the trumpet well enough I could acquire a special status among the Scouts and get to march next to the columns during their parades. The crowd on the streets would notice me, and who knows? Marika might be among them.

My parents declined to pay for an instructor because I had given up studying the piano, so I taught myself as well as I could. I was quite musical but I took great pains to discover the proper technique as I practiced day after day. I wasn't terribly good but was surprised how much I learned without professional help. After a few weeks I could blow sounds that were not too far from acceptable. The neighbors began to complain to my parents, however, and so they soon put an end to my career as a bugle boy.

As a Scout I had enjoyed the weekend hikes; they made me feel good physically. I also liked the fresh air and the exposure to nature, its threatening beauty and its serenity. I became familiar with the mountains of Buda.

One day our Boy Scout leader announced that we were going on a camping trip. It sounded exciting and romantic, something I had never done before. Irvin and I relished the idea of getting away from home and staying up in the mountains.

Like many ideas, which sound great in theory, this one proved sorely disappointing in practice. The moment we arrived at our campsite and began to pitch our tents and dig holes in the ground for the latrines, I started to miss the comforts of home. The war experience was still very vivid in my memory and it seemed I was reliving it. For one thing, our tents were very primitive. They didn't have canvas bottoms; we had to cover the dirt with a blanket. The first morning, after a horrible night of worries about bugs, worms and spiders crawling on me, I had a quick talk with Irvin, who shared my feelings. We decided to leave without telling our leader. Instead, we left word with a kid that we felt sick and had to go home. That was the last camping experience of my life.

Not long after, I became disappointed with the activities of the Boy Scouts. I found the meetings silly and childish and too military for my taste. I was more interested in pursuing my science studies. Every week I bought *Science Magazine*, a popular periodical in Budapest at the time, and read it from cover to cover. There was a series of articles on the building of the atom bomb that I found tremendously exciting. I learned something about chain reactions and nuclear fusion and never thought about the moral implications. I had the focused curiosity of a student who knew already what he wanted to become in life. I was determined to become a scientist.

The Boy Scouts organization didn't survive very long in Hungary. The following year, when the Communist Party came to power, the new government banned the Scouts, claiming they were a capitalist military organization. They replaced them immediately with the Üttörök, a communist youth organization structured along the same lines as the Scouts. They changed the color of the uniforms from khaki to blue and white, and the scarves from green to red. The meetings, of course, turned into ideological indoctrinations. I didn't even consider joining them; I had had enough of organizations and the company of boys. I wanted to be with girls and with my books and experiments.

Since the shower adventure I had run into Marika a few times but nothing dramatic had happened. I sensed a slight aloofness on her part and interpreted it immediately as a bad sign. I presumed she had found a boyfriend and didn't care about me anymore. Those thoughts disturbed me profoundly. I went to sleep every night tormented by the vision of her wonderfully shaped behind. I was desperate to make love to her. At the same time, I started dreaming of erotic adventures and having nocturnal emissions. In the mornings I was embarrassed by my stained pajamas. Also, it looked like I was masturbating. Kids talked about masturbation a lot in school but I didn't want to do anything less than fuck Marika.

One oppressively dull day, the kind in which the mind turns inward to protect itself from the prevailing atmospheric gloom, I came upon another inspired idea. I rushed next door to the Toths, though not without some apprehension because it had been a while since I had seen Marika last, and I asked her if she would come hiking with me Sunday. I told her I knew most of the trails in the nearby mountains of Buda and that she wouldn't have to worry about getting lost. I had maps and a compass, and she knew I used to be a Scout. She loved the idea.

The following days turned out to be the longest week of my life. I was praying for the weather to be nice and warm. I wouldn't have been able to cope with a rainy Sunday after the long build up during the week.

When I got up early Sunday morning I rushed to the window to check the weather. It was a perfect day. But the night before I suffered nightmares of rain in the morning and Marika canceling the trip, saying she couldn't come the weekend after either because she had already made plans with her boyfriend to visit a fair.

My mother was already in the kitchen preparing my breakfast and packing some lunch into the tiny bag I always carried fastened to my belt. Most Scouts schlepped heavy shoulder bags and backpacks and moaned and groaned throughout our hiking trips. Even then, I liked to travel lightly and elegantly.

Marika and I took the number six streetcar. It was nearly empty. Only a few laborers in their Sunday best and some old ladies in dark dresses traveled at this hour on a Sunday. We sat next to one another and talked about school, work and the atom bomb. She pretended to be interested in my account of chain reactions. I believed I was explaining it badly so quickly changed the subject to Communism. That wasn't a clever choice of subject matter, either.

It was a long journey to the mountains. We had to transfer twice before reaching the end of the line. I was worried that eventually we would run out of subjects to discuss. It felt good sitting next to her on the narrow bench; our knees touched once in a while when the streetcar made a sharp turn and I was inspired with wild erotic fantasies. She wore a pretty blue skirt and white cotton sweater; girls in those days didn't wear blue jeans or pants.

By the time we got off the third streetcar we ran out of conversation. The closer we got to the mountains the more silent I became. Once in a while, when I spotted a flower in the grass whose Latin name I knew, I blurted it out, much to her amazement, or occasionally named a few mountains in the distance I remembered from my Scout days.

At the same time I was scheming, trying to think up ways to get her to make love to me. I was hoping that she would attack me with deep passion and introduce me to the pleasures of love.

We started off at Huvosvolgy ("Cool Valley" in literal translation) and hiked on familiar paths I knew well from earlier outings. We walked for hours on our way to a lookout where we could rest and eat our lunch. She picked some wild flowers on our way and by the time we reached our destination she had gathered a huge bouquet. I couldn't come up with any feasible ideas during that period so I decided to forget about making love and just enjoy the outing. I wasn't happy about the decision at all.

She had brought along a small blanket which she spread out on the grass. We settled down for our *dejeuner sur l'herbe*. I took my lunch out of my hip pouch—a sandwich and an apple—and she added her boiled eggs and salami on bread. We shared and enjoyed the spread. I was famished.

Once in a while, as she reached for the food, I took a glance at her bare legs.

My fantasies started up again. By the time we finished lunch I was aroused and came upon a brilliant idea.

After we cleared the blanket and put the leftovers away, we lay on our backs enjoying the sun and the rest. I began rehearsing a speech in my mind and waited for the perfect moment to deliver it. I looked at her. Her eyes were closed. I asked her if she was sleepy. She said it was just the sun and that she was feeling good. I decided this was the moment when I must tell her what I had on my mind or I would never see her again and would curse myself for the rest of my life.

After some inner struggle, I confessed to her that whenever I was in her company I became aroused and ended up with a tremendous stomachache. I used the word "stomach" instead of "groin" to be discreet. She opened her eyes and sat up looking at me with a smile I had never before seen on her face. She asked me if I had an erection. I nodded my head, and with a superhuman effort I blurted out the question I had been wanting to ask for a long time, if she would make love to me. She laughed. She said I was too young, and that she had never done it before, and would only do it with someone much older. She leaned over to me and whispered that we could do something close to it. She asked me to close my eyes. I did so. A moment later I felt her warm hand slip up my leg, under my shorts. She didn't stop until she reached my erect penis. Slowly, she masturbated me, and at the same time, kept asking if I liked it. I couldn't utter a word. It was all new to me, and wonderful. She cleaned me up with her handkerchief and said I had just lost my virginity. It was fun all right, but I knew, and she admitted it wasn't the real thing. She promised me that in a few years she would teach me how to do it the real way. For the time being I was happy but slightly confused. The outing could have turned out worse.

* * *

IX.

THE SANTA ANA winds are still blowing in the southland, spreading brush fires in the San Bernadino mountains and some parts of the Hollywood Hills. The dry grass burns like napalm from the fury of the winds. No one can tell whether the fires are caused by human negligence or some mysterious force of nature. The burning bushes offer no revelations to the inhabitants of the Hollywood Hills, who have been waiting for a divine sign all their lives.

The water supply is getting "dangerously low," according to last night's newscast. Some Cassandras are predicting that this heat wave is a presage of "the big one," as if Hollywood didn't have enough man-made disasters.

An actors' strike is looming. The industry is nearly paralyzed. There is a lot of time for self-reflection and for polishing existing scripts. Perhaps the current situation will improve the next batch of screenplays. Such minor disasters often help temporarily to eliminate garbage.

These fragmented thoughts flash through my mind as I sit at my desk with my feet resting on *Webster's Ninth New Collegiate Dictionary*. The central air-conditioner is blowing stale, cool air over my head, contaminating the place with who-knows-what.

I take a glimpse at my watch. It is four in the afternoon. I must plan for the rest of the day. Since my disastrous lunch with Cass yesterday I have been weighing my options. None of them is promising. I won't give up, of course, but I should consider the unlikelihood of achieving my goal, though it is not in my nature to make realistic choices. I am going to follow Cass home.

I put on jeans and tennis shoes and walk to her office on Wilshire Boulevard. The streets are nearly devoid of pedestrians at this hour.

I sit on a bench at a bus stop across from the medical building and bury my head in the *Los Angeles Times* just as I have seen it done in the movies. I don't know why, but I am certain she will emerge on foot from the building at five o'clock. I didn't dare call her office to find out at what time she leaves work. I didn't want to arouse her suspicions with mysterious phone calls.

The rush-hour traffic started an hour ago. I am feeling slightly faint from the carbon monoxide but I refuse to leave my watch post; if she works until five she will be out in a few minutes. She is not the type to linger on after hours chatting and gossiping with her secretary. I am curious what color she will be wearing today. White again? Does she wear a different color every day or insist on white no matter what her mood is in the morning?

At ten minutes past five, Cass rushes out of the office building and heads in the direction she came from the day I first saw her. My blood pressure rises and aggravates the headache I have developed from the exhaust fumes.

I begin to follow her from across the street until I reach a crosswalk at a traffic light. She seems to be in a hurry–the disease of most urban professionals.

It is easy to follow her purposeful walk. She never turns around. At Dayton I cross to the other side of the street and keep at least twenty yards between us. I am enjoying myself. I feel like a naughty child again, involved in a forbidden game, quite innocent at the moment, but not completely free of danger either. At Palm Drive she turns right and continues until she reaches a four-story condominium. She enters without glancing behind her. So far, all has worked out well. She must be single; if she were married with children she would be living in a house. Well, it is not quite as simple as that. Being a professional, she could be married without children and live in a condo. At her age that is the most likely possibility.

I wait a few minutes until she fetches her mail and calls for the elevator. It should not take long. I check the time, I don't know why; it is twenty-five minutes to six. I walk up and down the street a few minutes, then ring the apartment of the Superintendent.

"Yes," says a grumpy male voice.

"Do you have any units for sale?"

"We've got two for sale. You wanna see them?"

"I'd like to, yes," I say eagerly.

"I'll come and let you into the lobby," he says and hangs up. Shortly after, the superintendent steps out of the elevator, looking just the way he sounded on the intercom. It is disappointing that most people fall naturally into stereotypes.

"One or two bedrooms?" he asks before pressing one of the buttons on the floor panel in the elevator.

"Show me the two-bedroom unit, please," I say without hesitation.

"That's on the third," he says, and we're on our way. He leads me into an unfurnished apartment, large and well built. The floor is elegant dark parquet; no wall-to-wall carpets here.

"Someone I know recommended this building. I think her name is . . . Atwill, Dr. Atwill," I say, acting silly for the janitor, or just worried that he might mention my visit to Cass when he sees her.

"Oh, yeah. She's a fine lady," he says with reverence. "She lives right above this one, on the fourth."

"Really? She lives alone, I believe, doesn't she?" I ask innocently, continuing my acting lesson.

"She does. She's too smart for men, I figure." He laughs, showing a missing tooth.

"I guess, she is. You're right," I say as I walk into one of the bedrooms. "A nice place you've got here."

"They're all beautiful, these units," he says with pride.

"Give me the rental-office number and I'll call them tomorrow."

He hands me a business card.

"What's your name again, Sir?" he asks as if it were his business to know.

One of those stupid customs. Now I have to continue the series of lies. I must be careful to give him a foreign sounding name. Most people believe, or so they tell me, that my accent is fine and charming, that it makes me unique, and that I shouldn't worry about it. But I do. After decades I still have a Hungarian accent and I hate it. It contributes to my insecurity in speaking English. I am never sure if I use enough colloquialisms in my speech, and I always have to concentrate on using the right pronoun. The Hungarian language doesn't distinguish between "he" and "she".

"Thomas Fekete is the name. I'll be in touch with the office. Thank you for showing me the place."

"Do you want to see the other one, too?"

"No, thanks. I like this one."

The Superintendent locks the apartment as I call for the elevator. While waiting, I consider the possibility that Cass may decide to go out and will be in the elevator I just called down. I break out in a cold sweat; I can actually feel the beads of perspiration ooze out on my forehead just below my hairline and in my armpits. It is very quick; the body reacts instantly to danger.

I fear coincidences and I fear being surprised by them. They are everywhere around us, haunting us with their irony and unpredictability, frightening and, at the same time, lucky phenomena, the cousins of fortune and disaster. You may count on them to happen when you become conscious of their plausibility. It is not impossible at all that I will find Cass in the elevator. How would she react upon seeing me? To her, it would not be serendipity. She would throw a fit and call the cops to report that I was stalking her and harassing her. That would be the end of my pursuit, not to mention my career.

The elevator door opens, interrupting my reveries. There is no one inside. As we step into the elevator I detect a familiar scent in the air, very faint but unmistakably Cass's. Did she just leave a minute ago or is it the residual of her riding up fifteen minutes ago? We descend in silence.

In the lobby I say good-bye to the janitor and leave with an accelerated heartbeat and a question mark in my mind. What am I going to do next, and when am I going to do it?

I walk all the way home. In Los Angeles one cannot hail a cab on the streets. You have to phone for one, or pick one up at a hotel. Mostly tourists and old women take cabs. Public transportation here is shamefu¹ disgustingly filthy, and often dangerous. It is relegated t working class, the homeless, and the crazies. The mid... a bus in this city, since it means sitting next to a member of the and breathing the air of stale farts and diesel fumes.

I stop at a florist on Santa Monica Boulevard to buy a bouquet of red carnations for Phoebe. They operated on her nose this morning. Next to roses, which I don't want to give her because of their obvious romantic overtones, my favorite flower is the carnation, the symbol of Hungarian revolutions. It was my father's favorite flower too. He used to send my mother red carnations every year for their anniversary. On their last one she received forty-eight stems. Not long after that, he died and six months after that, my mother followed with a broken heart.

Like most Americans, I take showers. The piercing hot water relaxes the muscles and induces a quasi-soporific state of mind, similar to being on the threshold of sleep when wild and fresh ideas emerge from the subconscious—sometimes even good ones. I don't understand why hot showers do that to me, but they prepare me emotionally for the unpredictability of the day. This could explain why good ideas pop into my mind in the shower stall. Of course, this theory doesn't apply to the evening shower I am taking now; this one is for purely hygienic reasons.

I dress and drive to Cedars Sinai Hospital.

Phoebe is alone in her room with tubes sticking out of her mouth and arm. She looks like an enormous retort. It is not a pretty sight. As I carefully place the flowers on the bedside table, I notice her eyes open. She tries to smile. I reach for her hand and she seems to appreciate my touch, however tentative. My eyes rest on her bandaged nose and I consider instantly of the possibility that she might be allergic to carnations. It wouldn't be pleasant for her to start sneezing in her condition.

I can't wait to get out of this room, this hospital. The smell, the sight, the overwhelming presence of pain and death scare me. I am fighting the images that come to mind: the surgeon with his scalpel, the decaying human body.

I am sure she doesn't want visitors to linger. I kiss her forehead and leave.

Out on the street I take a deep breath of the filthy air and remind myself w courageous women are when confronted with physical pain.

Cass's face pops into my mind and I forget quickly about Phoebe. What should the next step be to assure some progress in my pursuit? It is approximately seven-thirty now; she is probably going out to dinner about this time on a Thursday evening. A professional woman of her class wouldn't have a solitary dinner at home every day. By the end of the week she would be fed up with staying at home alone and eating an omelet or some pasta. It is time to start socializing; leave Monday, Tuesday and maybe Wednesday for loneliness.

I head over to Palm Drive and park far enough from her apartment building so that she will be unlikely to see my car. I switch on the radio to catch the tail end of the news: the Palestinians are demonstrating against the Israelis; British soldiers are killed by a car bomb in Belfast; sex scandal in the White House; the French are being difficult again at international conferences; and gang members kill a twelve year old girl in a drive-by shooting in Los Angeles. In other words, nothing new at all.

What kind of news do I want to hear, anyway? That researchers at UCLA have discovered the genes that control good and evil in humans? What if it becomes possible one day to control good and evil? Do we really want to live in the Garden of Eden? Perhaps a healthy dose of evil is necessary. We need the drama to energize our actions and our imaginations, conflict to create works of art and discover the mechanics of our universe. What a bore life would be without evil. But how much evil is good? What about the genocides throughout history? The Holocaust in our time? Were they necessary? And how can we avoid such inhuman atrocities in the future without having full control over evil?

Before I ask myself more questions, I switch to classical music. Mendelssohn's Piano Concerto No. 1, one of my favorite piano concertos, is playing. It puts me in a better mood and makes me oblivious to the world outside. Only music of all the arts has such an effect on the human mind.

It is close to eight o'clock and almost dark. The garage door rolls up with an irritating noise and Cass's elegant BMW heads toward Wilshire Boulevard. I start my car and follow her from a safe distance. She is probably meeting her boyfriend for dinner and that will be the end of this evening's adventure. She glides through Beverly Hills, crosses over to Melrose Avenue, Hollywood's trendy shopping strip, and heads east toward Paramount Studios.

Doubts about my behavior nag at me as I keep following her car to its unknown destination, but some enigmatic force keeps me on her tail. What am I going to do when I get there? I have no idea.

In the heart of Hollywood, at the corner of Martel and Melrose, she stops at a fashionable Italian restaurant, La Cucina. The place is informal, always full and frequented mostly by the music and film crowd. I continue on, passing another Italian restaurant, Angeli, a few blocks further east. I park on a side street, not too far from Melrose, and walk to Angeli. This area at night is not safe for lone pedestrians.

The wonderful smell of Italian spices tickles the allergy-prone membranes in my nose and I begin to sneeze violently, three or four times without pause, as the waitress shows me to a small table near the pizza oven. I order a glass of red wine and a pizza with sausage and green peppers. The place is packed with a colorful crowd: musicians with long red, platinum and green hair and funky clothes emphasizing sexual ambiguity; punks, even more offensive to middle class sensibilities in their getups and Mohawk hairdos; and young actors and actresses in tight jeans looking sexy and hopeful. It is a hip neighborhood with shops and restaurants catering to this young crowd.

I hate dining alone. It reminds me of old age, lonely widowers, desperation. Right now I am too preoccupied with formulating my next move to be concerned with loneliness or boredom. I have not come up with a fabulous plan for the rest of the evening, so I will have to keep adjusting my actions according to the situation I confront or create, which most likely will turn out differently from what I anticipate.

After dinner I will walk by La Cucina and try to spot her through the window; I am curious what her boyfriend looks like. If I recall, the restaurant is paneled with large, curtained windows that look out on Melrose. From the dark street I should be able to see inside without being noticed by the patrons in the restaurant.

I gobble down my pizza in a hurry, pay and leave.

The last few days, the Santa Ana winds have kept the nights unusually warm.

I decide, at first, just to walk by quickly and show only my profile to the windows. If I can't spot her from the corner of my eye I will pass by again more slowly, or even stop and pretend to read the menu on display.

When I reach the window I spot her immediately. She is seated at a round table in the corner next to the window in the company of three women. They all look like professionals–probably her colleagues. I am relieved. At least she is not with a man. Not that I am jealous, or have the right to be jealous.

The image of Cass behind the tulle curtain, eating, talking, and laughing with her friends activates a strong physical desire in me. I am burning inside with the intensity I used to feel for Marika. Her smell, her touch, her voice calling my name, the taste of sweat on her skin, the sight of her figure and her blondness are unforgettable and I am desperate to experience them again.

As the years go by, the senses dull to a less sensitive state. Once in a while, a phrase of music or a whiff of smell transports me back to the past accompanied by a quickened heartbeat–that's about all. The discovery of the realm of the senses is over after adolescence. What we believe to be in our adulthood a new sensual experience is merely an artificially intensified or induced sensation we already know and have experienced before. It is not accompanied by the jolts of discovery, which are so extraordinarily beautiful in our youth; that affirmation of life, the acute consciousness as the self enters into a new phase–into manhood. What a pity it doesn't last longer. Preparation for death begins at an early age.

I return to my car without knowing what I will do next. I don't want to go home, that much I know. On my way west on Beverly Boulevard I decide to drive to Cass's condo. I am still not sure why, but I begin to imagine confrontations both on the street and in her apartment. How am I going to manage these? The only possible way is to park close to the garage door and follow her inside when it opens. She will think I am a tenant who is too lazy to get out the garage key.

She may be scared if I do that but I have to take the risk. Life becomes unbearably stale without taking risks. Yes, that is my problem. I have been living a stale existence lately. I sold out to the Philistines. I haven't created a film worth watching for a long time. Why? Because I haven't lived dangerously enough, I haven't taken chances. I've been afraid of losing my middle-class status. How ridiculous! Well, if I consider what my lifestyle used to be in Communist Hungary it is not surprising at all that I became preoccupied with consumerism in North America. But I thought I had shed my bourgeois tendencies some time ago. Yes, I had for a while, but they sneaked back upon me imperceptibly. I became friends with some producers in Canada and their influence rubbed off on me. I listened to them, I wanted my films to make money. I succumbed to the temptation, I sacrificed my artistic ambitions for loyalty to these people. I am paying dearly for it now.

My first full-length feature film was made with passion and integrity. It became Canada's official entry to the Cannes Film Festival in 1969 and garnered good reviews but didn't make money. I was disillusioned and had a hard time selling quality projects. That is the reason I let myself be seduced into making commercial films. Ironically, those commercial films weren't successful at the box office either. So, I lost both battles one after the other.

But I am going to change the course of my life; I have the will power. I will do everything I can to regain my dignity as a filmmaker, as an artist. I am going to take chances; I will make films about life, not silly dreams for Hollywood mass consumption. How could I have been so short-sighted for so long, so blinded by the irresponsible promises of those people? In the end, they let you down anyway. If you don't make money for them they forget friendship, they betray you. My life is a series of betrayals by so-called friends who climbed to positions on the top of my back. Now, I am in the process of changing; I am on the right track. It will begin with Cass. I must succeed with her and then everything will fall into place.

I have been sitting in my car for hours when her BMW turns the corner of Palm and Wilshire. I have fewer than five seconds to decide whether to follow her into the garage or go home. I decide to take the chance. I start my car and slip through just before the gate rolls shut in the small, dimly lit garage. I park in an empty space designated for a tenant, near where she parked. Cass looks around as she locks the car and notices me immediately. She tries to hide her shock but I can see her eyes widen as I approach her, a reflex reaction of humans ready to flee.

"Don't be scared, Cass," I say as calmly as I can. "I just came to invite you out for a nightcap."

"You have an odd way of inviting women out for drinks," she says with an unsteady voice. "Why didn't you call me at the office? Sneaking up on me at night in the garage is not the style I expect from men."

I take a step forward so I can lower my voice. "I didn't think you'd take my call. That's why I decided to wait for you in front of your building."

"How did you find out where I live?"

"It wasn't difficult."

"What do you want, Gabi?" she asks firmly, trying to gain control of the situation.

"I want to take you for a drink, that's all," I say, and wait. For a second she resists but then thinks better of it and follows me to my car.

What went through her mind? Why has she decided to follow me without too much resistance? Perhaps she thinks it will calm me down and avert a confrontation, physical or verbal. Or, has she started to relax her understandable prejudice toward me? Could she be getting used to the idea of loving me?

On our way to the Polo Lounge she only asks where we are going. I don't want to force a conversation, some silly small talk that leads nowhere. I decide to stay quiet.

The headwaiter takes us to a comfortable booth across from the bar. She orders an Armagnac, I order a Calvados again.

"Do you believe in God, Gabi?" she asks without any lead-in to this awkward but shrewd question.

"I've been thinking about it, a lot, I must say," I fumble, "I am inclined toward . . . not believing in God as a theological concept . . . I'm closer to being an agnostic than an atheist, I think. It's a hard question to answer . . . Perhaps I am hovering between an agnostic and an atheist. That comes the closest to your question."

"Have you ever wondered what would happen if one day a scientist came up with a theory, an equation, which proved the existence of God, that he, she, it, created the universe just an instant before the *big bang?*" she asks, relaxed now. Another odd question, and she assumes I am familiar with the big bang theory. What is she driving at? I suppose I will find out soon.

"Yes, it'd be wonderful, but I don't think the knowledge will necessarily improve mankind. God, if He exists at all, will be indifferent to our world on this planet and to the individual human beings anyway. Our awareness of this new theory, assuming someone does come up with it one day, will not change God's mind about humanity. Just consider what has taken place in history so far. My belief is that the universe wasn't created at all, but has been in existence and will be in existence indefinitely. Of course, this is only a wild guess on my part. For me, the real question is, if we take the existence of God for granted why did God create the universe in the first place, and for what purpose? On the other hand, if God didn't have a purpose for us humans, we must find purpose in our lives ourselves. Otherwise life is completely useless, a waste of energy and suffering. It doesn't seem to me, considering again the existence of a superior Creator, that Earth is God's favorite planet. If it were, God wouldn't have populated it with humans."

"That's not an overly optimistic world view, is it?" she says between sips of her drink.

"It's not entirely pessimistic either. Making movies gives me the opportunity to create a better world on the screen, an ideal world which should be taken seriously but isn't. Few people take art seriously enough to be changed by it. And I am not even sure that's the purpose of art anyway." I am wondering how pompous it all sounds.

"You directors, you like playing God, don't you?" She says shrewdly. I instantly realize that she's testing me for illusions of grandeur. Does she think I believe I'm Jesus Christ?

"Not only directors, but all artists believe that the most gratifying human experience is creativity," I say defensively.

"But directors enjoy exerting more control over their associates than most other creative professionals, don't you think so?"

"They have to. But that's not part of the creative work, that's just a practical necessity, controlling a large crew and an army of actors." I must get out of this line of argument. I have to change the subject otherwise we'll be sitting here until breakfast discussing the existence of God. "Just one last word on the subject," I say with finality. "If we believe in the premise that God created the universe, we must also ask the question, who created God?" She doesn't say a word, just stares in front of her. I've got to do something radical right now. She is sitting quietly next to me on an upholstered bench, semi-circular in shape, sipping the amber-colored Armagnac. I know what I will do.

As she puts her fat snifter down on the gray marble table I lean over and quickly kiss her on the mouth. It happens so fast that she is unable to stop me or turn away from me. When she recovers from the initial shock, Cass disengages herself from my adolescent embrace.

"Gabi, you can't go on behaving like an oversexed child." She doesn't sound angry, only disturbingly patronizing. At least she didn't slap my face in public.

"Artists are children, you know that."

"Only when you create, not in public in the company of a woman."

"They are either consistently childish in every situation or they are not at all. They don't switch back and forth."

"Gabi, you're so full of it," she sighs with a touch of amusement in her voice. "I know what you want, and I also told you that I am not game. Why don't you live with the facts of life and find another woman who looks like Marika and fuck *her*?" I am taken aback by the sudden change of tone in her language; she is obviously becoming impatient with me.

"Because I want you," I say gently, lovingly. "I must have *you*."

"What if you can't have me? What are you going to do?"

"I haven't decided yet, but you don't have to worry. I won't harm you."

"That's reassuring," she sneers. "I think it's time to go." She suddenly rises and leaves me at the table. I don't know what to do first: pay the check or run after her. I can feel the eyes of strangers on me waiting for my next move. I decide to stay for a few more minutes and pretend she left for the washroom. But they may have heard her voice raised. What do I care? Concern for public opinion is a petit bourgeois preoccupation. This is ridiculous. When the waiter passes by my table I ask for the check.

The next morning a large earthquake, 5.3 on the Richter scale, wakes me at seven o'clock. My apartment on the fourteenth floor swings dangerously, and I hear loud screeching noises. I jump out of bed and rush under a doorway as I learned to do from watching a TV show on how to survive an earthquake. The experience reminds me of the war years when bombs were falling all around us, shaking our building, threatening to collapse it. In a few seconds, the earthquake is over without any perceptible damage to the apartment. It wasn't the *big one* that scientists have predicted will happen within thirty years. Still, it is not the ideal way to start the day.

I amble out into the kitchen and put on the kettle for coffee. Despite everything that is ugly in the world, it is good to be alive. One needs a serious reminder once in a while of the real values of life. While sipping my orange juice

I look up a florist in the Yellow Pages and order a dozen red roses to be sent to Cass's apartment with a note saying, "Let's have dinner this time."

I haven't been behind the camera for months and my bank account is drying out. I am not only going through a creative and emotional crisis but also a financial one.

I take the coffee beans out of the fridge and grind enough for two cups. I need that much to get me going today.

I am carrying my cereal bowl and coffee to the dining area and can't help glancing at the mirror in the hallway. I notice a new crease above my upper lip, probably caused by sleeping on it. In a few hours it will be gone, I am sure, but in a year or less there will be a permanent line there, showing the inevitable weakness of the flesh against wear and tear. I try to console myself by thinking that the problems I complain about are minuscule compared to most people's miseries.

All these self-examinations suddenly disgust me. I shift my thoughts from myself to Phoebe. I am wondering how she is. The poor girl, I hope she is not in too much pain. I will call her in the hospital after I have finished breakfast, I may even visit her this morning. She would be happy to see someone at this hour.

When I call the hospital room the switchboard intercepts with Phoebe's message: She doesn't want to take calls or see visitors for the next few days. She must look beat up after surgery; it is understandable that she would rather be alone in her condition.

I step out onto the balcony overlooking the sound stages on the Fox lot to finish my coffee. The sight disturbs me. I have never made an in-house studio picture.

It is still unbearably hot from the Santa Ana winds, and according to the news report on the radio that filters through my balcony door, the smog factor is high enough to be dangerous to people with respiratory diseases and allergies. I start sneezing on cue. Balancing my cup and saucer, I return to the living room.

I have to decide whether to call Cass now or wait until she reacts to the bouquet of flowers I sent her. Instead, I sit down in the living room to watch the Wimbeldon quarter finals on cable TV till noon. Later I may go out to lunch with one of my writer friends if I can find someone free on such short notice.

I haven't felt so lonely since I moved from Canada. I have made a few new friends here but I am not certain how deep my friendships are, how loyal these friends will be when it comes to the crunch. It is hard to make life-long friends at my age. When a person becomes successful overnight in Hollywood, he instantly finds himself in a different crowd and terminates his old friendships, unless the person is made of an unusually strong moral fiber. I helped a few actors become stars but they don't return my calls these days because I haven't directed a successful film for a while. I understand their behavior; I would be more surprised if they acted differently.

Humans are pathetic when viewed from the grand perspective. One day we pop out of our mother's belly and as soon as we are able to think the first idea that comes to us is of our importance in the world. This childish self-centeredness prevails among the so-called adults in Hollywood. From a distance, they are amusing to watch, but when you are involved with these people at work their lack of insight into themselves becomes irritating. They are overly concerned with their positions, with empire building and the joy of power.

A few days after I sent the flowers, Cass writes me a thank you note, declining politely my dinner invitation: "I am too busy professionally and socially these days to make an extra effort to dine out with you," she writes among a few other things not worth mentioning. I must devise new tactics that don't offend or frighten her. I may have made a major mistake the other night surprising her in the garage. It was in poor taste and could have been construed as psychotic behavior. It must have seemed to her as a desperate attempt at seduction. Women don't like desperate men, I know that. Why don't I think before I act? No more impulsive behavior.

I call the florist to deliver one red rose to her office every day for the remainder of the week. I shouldn't be spending all this money on luxuries at a time when I can't afford them. Well, it is only money, as the saying goes. I can always find some work in TV when the going gets rough in the feature industry.

Next day I call Cedars Sinai Hospital again. This time a sleepy sounding Phoebe picks up the phone.

"I've been trying to reach you for the past few days," I say without introduction.

"Yes, I know. My face looks like a Jackson Pollock. I kept everyone away, even my parents. If my father saw me like this he'd ask for the death penalty at the trial."

"Have you forgiven that punk already?"

"No, I haven't. I'll do my own punishing when the time comes. I don't have to rely on our dubious justice system. I've got my ways, don't worry," Her voice is without emotion. I am wondering what is in store for the punk: castration, or some psychological torture only a woman knows how to inflict?

"I *am* worried. You shouldn't bother with him anymore," I say, probably sounding like her father.

"What are you doing with yourself these days?" she asks, more cheerful now.

"In what area do you mean?"

"Are you getting laid by some cine-sluts?"

"I'm not promiscuous these days, you know that."

"No, I don't know that."

"You're not jealous, are you?" I say, and regret it. She's been screwing her boyfriend and has the nerve to ask me about other women I may fuck while she is suffering.

"I'm not. I just don't want to worry about AIDS."

"Speaking of AIDS. Did you get any blood transfusions during the surgery?"

"For God's sake, Gabi. This was a minor operation; it only looks like a major fuck-up. I was getting salt water, they said. I'd have given them my own blood if I needed a transfusion. I asked them before the surgery."

"That was smart of you."

"Well, what do you expect?" she says indignantly. "I'll be at home tomorrow but I don't want to see you until I am presentable. It'll take a week or so before the blood is absorbed under the skin."

"I'll be waiting for you patiently. Take care!"

"You too. I'll call when I'm ready for society." She hangs up.

I can't help admiring the way she springs back to life after surgery and pain. Women are remarkable creatures: they are resilient and possess common sense. They rule the world. In a few decades men will become second-class citizens, at least in the United States; it is time for them to experience that condition.

I am restless. Cass drives me around the bend with her militant resistance. And Phoebe is out of my life for a while. I don't want to start another superficial relationship for the sake of getting laid. I must exercise self-discipline. Also, I need work. My agent tells me everyone is out of work; the impending strike is ruining the industry.

I spend the rest of the day reading and thinking about new ideas.

Dinnertime is approaching and I haven't yet lined up anyone to listen to my bitching about the industry and the state of the arts. It is Cass I want for dinner and after dinner. She'd better change her ideas about me by the end of the week. I will call her Friday and suggest a weekend trip to Santa Barbara. She may come along. What if she won't? I should be prepared for failure but it is not my style. This seduction game could go on forever without results. I can't imagine an irreversible rejection; it must be just a question of time and strategy. If I handle it shrewdly I will succeed.

As I slip into bed a deep sense of loneliness overcomes me. I find it increasingly difficult to go to bed at night alone. I should get married. I am weary of bachelorhood with its unlimited opportunities and unpredictable choices. I am slipping back to middle-class values, and why not? Some of the middle-class values are not all that bad. Family, for instance, is important, even for a creative person. Some of the greatest artists were bourgeois at heart. Not all artists are social rebels. There is no use trying to justify my artistic crisis as a product of living a middle-class existence. Originality, style, and a universal vision cannot be contaminated by family life. Perhaps my personality isn't that of the radical artist. But again, the artist should be radical in his art, not in his interaction with people and society.

Should I ask Cass to marry me?

* * *

X.

AFTER OUR HÜVÖSVÖLGY adventure I didn't see Marika for a long while. It occurred to me that she was probably embarrassed by what had transpired and didn't want to continue our friendship for fear of going too far with a young boy. Most likely, she believed I could handle it by myself now that she had shown me how to do it. I went through agonies thinking about the experience. I reconstructed every little detail of the outing in my mind like a criminal going over his crime again and again. The result was more pain in my groin.

When Marika and I met again accidentally on the staircase she was pleasant and civil but aloof. She asked about school and my piano lessons and, to my painful surprise, about girlfriends. I told her I didn't have any and didn't know where to find them.

I studied less and less in order to spend more time on my experiments and to daydream about Marika and sex. I found out that she dropped out of school and joined her stepmother at the shoe factory across from our courtyard. She suddenly seemed to me a grown-up.

Marika's cool disregard for my feelings devastated me. I couldn't understand her. For years, she behaved as if she loved me and was just waiting for me to grow up before finally making love to me. I felt at the time that I was already a grown-up, ripe for her love. I was in mental and physical torture over losing her.

One day, my brother grilled me with his usual bluntness about matters of the heart. When I didn't respond to his satisfaction, he asked me if I knew that Marika was screwing the janitor's son. He was a blue-collar worker in his twenties, living with his mother and sister in a depressing little shack in the middle of our courtyard. I couldn't imagine the object of my dreams making love with that nonentity. I was shattered, but secretly hoped that my brother wasn't telling me the truth, that he was just trying to make me get off my ass and look for a girlfriend.

I soon realized the hopelessness of dreaming about Marika and set out to find a girlfriend. Both decisions were easier said than done.

Irvin and I spent hours nearly every day walking the streets of Budapest in search of a girl. Our route was always the same: up on Rakoczy Boulevard, the busiest main artery, to the elegant center of the city which was the oldest part of Pest with its fashionable shops and cafés that I loved so much. We watched not only girls of our age but young women, too.

At the end of our frustrating and exhausting quest we routinely dropped into one of the cafés, called in Hungary *espressos*, and continued our scrutiny of women while sipping espresso coffee topped with a blob of whipped cream. I still miss those places with their tiny tables crowded in semi-darkness, smelling of strong coffee and cigarette smoke, promising romances with beautiful, sophisticated girls.

That was the time when I started smoking cigarettes. While drinking espressos in a café house and pretending to be an adult, smoking was a must and the most natural thing in the world for a young man on the make, except for Irvin—he was a good boy. Having developed a taste (in my imagination) for the good things in life at an early age, I smoked American cigarettes whenever

I could put my hands on some. They not only smelled wonderful but they were packaged beautifully compared to the local products. I hated Hungarian cigarettes; they were strong and smelled like forest fire. Also, in those days, it looked cool to smoke American cigarettes. My favorites were Phillip Morris and Camel. I got them on the black market across the street from our apartment.

Our neighborhood cinema, situated in a yellow two-story building at the corner of Istvan Boulevard and Bethlen Square, used to be called "Hollywood" before the Communist takeover in 1948. After that the officials changed it to the obvious, "Bethlen." It was right across from my elementary school and the synagogue where under the pressure from my religious grandfather I reluctantly performed the minimum requirements for my Bar Mitzvah.

Among the few pleasant memories of Budapest that traveled with me across the North Atlantic is that of the Bethlen movie theater, with its evergreen scented air freshener sprayed in the aisles between shows by a pretty usherette. That was where I first learned to love movies during and after school hours.

At the time, my favorite actors were Bogart and Eric von Stroheim. Most of their films were released in Hungary before 1948. And I was in love with Veronika Lake. For me, she embodied the ideal woman: the long, slightly wavy blonde hair covering her right eye; the slender, not too voluptuous body; the bluish gray eyes which, in moments of passion, projected warmth. I saw two or three films a week, mostly alone, sometimes with my friend Irvin.

Budapest was lively at that time; the economy was quite good. Hungarians loved living well and knew how to enjoy life. My brother owned a knitting firm but spent more time in bars and cafes than at his business. His ambition was to bed all the beautiful and available women in Budapest in a hurry. This compulsive behavior may have been a response to his experience in the Austrian concentration camp, where he wasted a few of his most valuable young years.

Some of the larger *espressos* in the center of town provided entertainment in the evenings, mostly singers accompanied by a pianist. One of the popular singers, a redhead, was my favorite; she was in her early twenties. For a while she became part of my fantasies until I found out one day that my brother was dating her. He was everywhere.

He must have noticed my desperate longing for girls because one day he offhandedly suggested I should go with my friend, Irvin, to a Five O'clock Tea dance at the immensely popular bar, the *Moulin Rouge*, an exact replica of the famous one in Paris where Toulouse-Lautrec used to hang out to draw and paint the patrons and the chorus girls.

In many important ways, Budapest was fashioned after Paris; between the two world wars it was called the Paris of Central Europe. The Opera House, some of the large boulevards, Heroes' Square and many other architectural landmarks are small-scale copies of their Parisian counterparts.

I didn't believe they would let us in a famous bar at our age but my brother assured me that if I told the doorman my name and referred to him, he would let us in.

I was thrilled to go, but Irvin wasn't too excited about our prospects or the idea itself. He couldn't dance, and I think he was afraid of his parents who started complaining that he spent too much valuable time with me.

By then, I had learned enough dance steps from Marika to take on the adventure and couldn't wait till Saturday afternoon. It would be my first visit to a notorious nightclub and the experience would help to cure me of Marika—I hoped.

I spent the rest of the week putting a wardrobe together. I was skinny but almost as tall as my brother and I could wear some of his clothes with minor alterations. He graciously gave me a pair of gray pants and a sports jacket for my induction into society. There was a tailor living on the first floor of our building who did minor alterations; in fact, that is all he did. Nobody in his right mind would have given him three meters of fine English fabric to have a suit made. He was a small, skinny guy, always smiling, polite to everyone, even to kids; he seemed terrified of the world.

I took my pants and jacket down and asked him to alter the pants into *pipe-pants*, fashionable for the young at that time. The jacket was almost perfect except for the sleeves and the shoulders. He said he could shorten the sleeves but didn't want to touch the shoulders. I didn't mind that too much for wide shoulders were also fashionable. The jacket looked like a zoot suit on me.

In a secondhand shoe shop I found a pair of pointed Italian shoes which were a size too large but looked good with my pants. They were black and white leather and reminded me of Fred Astaire movies; I laid newspaper on the inside soles to make them snug on my feet.

Friday afternoon I put on a dress rehearsal in front of the large bedroom mirror. It took me a while to figure out how to tie a Windsor knot on one of my brother's favorite silk ties.

My mother came into the bedroom unexpectedly. She didn't know how to react to the sight. However ridiculous I may have looked, she realized this was part of growing up in a family dominated by men. She stood behind me at the mirror, sort of smiled, and asked if the jacket wasn't a bit large. I said it was the fashion. She kept looking and shaking her head, perceptible only to me, and finally said I looked like a *yampetz,* which is Hungarian or Yiddish for *teddy boy.*

I cannot be sure whether that particular Saturday was sunny or overcast but my memory sees it as bright and beautiful.

The Moulin Rouge was situated in the best, most exciting part of the city, right in the center of the theatrical district. In fact, the same building also housed the Operetta Theater, the home of Lehar and Offenbach. The actual name of the street at that time was Nagymezö Street but everyone called it Broadway. Hungarians love copying success.

Anticipation of the dance was too much for me; I couldn't sleep or eat well for days. I didn't do any homework for a week. I believed that on Saturday I would enter the inner circle of grown-ups where sex and adventure were open to everyone easily and effortlessly. I felt my real Bar Mitzvah would happen Saturday in the Moulin Rouge.

Irvin was to pick me up at four o'clock. I was ready by three, sitting on pins and needles, leaning out the bedroom window, my cherished place for daydreaming. I watched the pedestrians, occasionally spat on them and waited for their surprised and angry reactions. At five to four I saw Irvin coming down the street. His gait was ponderous like that of most fat people burdened by the weight of bouncing blubber. I ran downstairs yelling, "good-bye," to my mother who was laboring, as always, in the kitchen, too resigned to see me off.

Irvin was dressed in his Sunday best, looking like an overfed choirboy with his rosy cheeks and blonde hair. He didn't look too happy or excited and didn't say a word until we arrived at Barros Square, near the railway station, to take a streetcar to the metro. While waiting for the streetcar he looked me over from top to bottom and said, "you look like a *yampetz*, just like your brother." I shrugged and said I needed something to attract girls.

Underground trains are intrinsically claustrophobia inducing. People scrutinize each other more there than in above-ground streetcars where they have the option of looking out the windows. Perhaps that is the reason why I felt everyone's eyes on my jacket and saw them snickering as they turned away from me. I started to sweat. By the time we got off at the corner of Andrassy Boulevard and Grand Circle Boulevard my shirt was soaked and so was my face. Irvin asked me how come I was perspiring so much when it was always he who did the sweating, and he was completely dry. I told him my jacket was too warm. He suggested that I take it off. I don't know why I hadn't thought of it myself.

We walked to Nagymezo Street and by four thirty we had arrived at the main entrance of the famous nightclub. I had cooled off by then and put my jacket back on. Probably because I had my brother as a reference I was able to fake some momentary self-confidence. We walked straight up to the doorman—Irvin tentatively trailing right behind me, hoping we would be turned down—and I told him rapidly that my brother had made arrangements to have us let in. He looked at me, smiled, and told us not to get drunk. We walked into the club.

It may have been the influence of seeing too many gangster films or my brother's lifestyle, but bars and nightclubs held a great fascination for me. They still do. At the time, they represented a world of adult sophistication, sex and decadence—a word I knew of but didn't fully understand. The Moulin Rouge lived up to my expectations.

As we entered, imbued with fear and reverence as in a child's first visit to a Gothic cathedral, I was struck immediately by the sweet smell of American tobacco, coffee, and French perfumes. They formed a heart-throbbing combination for a sensitive teenage nose reared on chemical experiments.

The club was built like a small cabaret theater with balconies, boxes and a stage. In the center of the main floor, surrounded by tables and chairs, was a parquet dance floor.

There was a long bar on the left with a row of red, upholstered stools. It was quite early but the bar was already packed with a well-dressed crowd—mostly young, underworld types and some familiar faces from the theater and the movies. I was deeply taken by the place and kept nudging Irvin, who either wasn't impressed at all, or was so intimidated that he put on a stoic attitude in self-defense.

A ravishing-looking girl with copper red hair stood behind the bar mixing cocktails. I often saw her window-shopping during my strolls on Vaci Street, the most fashionable street for shoppers and *espressos*. Those days in Budapest, bartenders were strictly gorgeous women, popular and known to the cognoscenti as are today's high-class fashion models.

As I stopped near the bar soaking up the sight and the smells, a sudden feeling of fulfillment spread over me, as if I had just crossed the threshold to adulthood. Irvin stood close to me in silence, his red face glowing like a giant apple.

It was light years away from my dreary everyday life. Everyone around us looked beautiful and well dressed. The furniture and walls were covered with burgundy red velvet and trimmed with gold. At that moment I understood my brother, and how easily any young person could be seduced by the sensuality of that environment.

A tall, imposing man in a tuxedo came over to us and politely asked if we wanted to have a table or stay at the bar. I nodded without fully understanding his question but he didn't need to hear our choice, he knew what we wanted and where we should sit.

So, we followed him to a small table in a box on the balcony. It was the first time in our lives that we were treated as adults and it was a revelation. As soon as the maitre'd left us, Irvin began to wonder if we would have enough money for the drinks and cover charges. I told him my brother had given me enough to pay the bill and that besides, they knew him well in case we ran into problems.

The musicians took their seats in the pit and started tuning their instruments. It was a big jazz band, a replica of the Glenn Miller orchestra. Its leader, "Csöppy" (a Hungarian term of endearment for a small person), was a short, bald man, witty and charming, and an excellent musician. Jazz was immensely popular in Hungary after the war and Csöppy was one of the best, if not the best band leader.

It was not quite five o'clock, but the floor and most of the boxes were already occupied by young couples and single guys anxious to swing to that exciting new sound from America. There weren't too many single girls, as far as I could see. Traditionally, they came in the company of a couple or in twos, never alone.

We didn't have to wait long before the waiter came around to take our order. My brother had suggested we drink a "White Lady" cocktail. We didn't know anything about cocktails; I suppose he didn't want us to get drunk on straight shots. I still remember its taste, bittersweet and sour, my first cocktail ever, served in a conical shaped glass I had never seen before. We were both impressed.

I hadn't drunk liquor since my Bar Mitzvah when I got drunk for the first and last time in my life. My only memory of that party on my thirteenth birthday is retching all afternoon. From then on, I never celebrated my birthdays.

At five sharp, Csöppy walked on the stage in his immaculate double-breasted, sky-blue suit and greeted his adoring audience with a few witty remarks about local politics. He started the music with a quick count down, tapping the floor with his right foot. "*In the Mood*" was the first number. Couples quickly filled the small rectangular dance floor, twirling and twisting, and performing minor acrobatics they had seen in some Hollywood pictures.

The respectful treatment we received from the waiters helped restore my self-confidence, and I began to scan the floor and the boxes for single girls. I was ready to give up when I discovered a pretty young woman sitting with a couple who were just getting up to go onto the dance floor. I informed Irvin, with the nonchalance of a hardened playboy, that I was going downstairs to ask her to dance. As I started to rise I noticed a guy, much older than I, already beating me to it. Irvin chuckled at my frustration.

I didn't have any prior experience in those matters but I was learning fast. I told Irvin I was going down anyway and would wait in the wings for the next number. I left him in the box sitting quietly with a lazy expression on his chubby face. He didn't like to make unnecessary moves.

Walking downstairs by myself I began to feel comfortable and confident and found my bearing easily. I stopped at a column near the staircase, leaned against it with my legs crossed, as if I had special privileges there, and searched for girls, particularly the one I had spotted before.

When the song finished, the dancers rushed back to their drinks to take a sip before the next number started, and to change partners if necessary. My eyes stopped on a blonde girl with bobbed hair being escorted back to her table by a man in his thirties. I hadn't seen her from above. She was seated right under our box in the company of two young couples. She was even prettier than the one I came down for, though a little bit on the heavy side—not fat or plump, just voluptuous. Hungarians called that type a *stuffed pigeon.* I liked her open expression and unadorned smile as she thanked her partner for the dance.

As I watched her the last image I had of Marika flashed through my mind. I couldn't help comparing Marika's new "adult" look with that girl who just finished dancing. I was wondering what would happen if Marika came here with her boyfriend and saw me dancing with that girl?

I decided to make my move. I didn't have to wait long before the band started their next number, "*An American Patrol.*" I took a deep breath, waited until my heartbeat calmed a little, and told myself the worst I could anticipate was a turndown, not an execution by a firing squad. I must do it. Before some shark beat me, I rushed to her table with quick steps and asked her to dance. She looked up without taking her full lips away from the champagne glass and glanced over at her friends, as if to ask them what she should do with this kid. Not receiving any encouragement from them, she placed her slender glass on the table and began to roll its stem with an expression that suggested either fatigue, or a feigned decadence.

Then, when I was ready to turn my back and walk away, her good nature got the better of her. She stood up, smiled at me gently, or condescendingly—I couldn't tell at the time—and to my great surprise, grabbed my hand and led me to the dance floor. Her hand was hot and soft; it felt like tiny cushions in my palm.

We began to dance, first tentatively, then with more confidence as I realized that I could lead quite well. I looked up to see if Irvin was watching. He was nodding his head in approval.

The girl was still overheated from the previous dance. I could smell her intoxicating body odor mixed with bath soap. I recognized immediately the familiar smell of *Caola* soap. My mother used it on occasions when she visited friends with my father. It was very expensive and lasted forever because she seldom used it.

Her eyes were unusually large and green. I stared at them in silence. I didn't know what to say to her, I was waiting for her to start the conversation but she didn't seem to care. The awkward silence made me sweat again and I began to panic. I didn't want her to see beads of perspiration on my forehead giving away my insecurities. I consoled myself with the excuse that it was inconvenient to talk during a fast number. We danced well and I was grateful to Marika that she had taught me the swing.

When the number was over my heart sank. It had been too brief to forge a connection and I figured she probably wouldn't dance with me again. But the music didn't stop; they segued into a slow number. She pulled me to her breast as we began the new piece. Her odors hit me in the face even more strongly. I was going to say something that I thought was a good opening line but when I opened my mouth I couldn't utter a word. A little later she asked what my name was. I was so confused that I told her my brother's name, then quickly corrected myself with some silly excuse that I was trying to remain incognito. She didn't know the word, which confused me even further, but she told me her name. It was Suzi. Encouraged, I asked her if she was interested in science. She said she wasn't; she wanted to become an actress. After that we didn't talk for a while.

During the dance I developed an erection despite the fact that I was tense and nervous. She must have noticed it, I thought, because she pressed her cheek against mine. At that moment I believed she would go to bed with me. Why would she press her face against mine if she hadn't fallen in love with me? I asked myself the logical question. I'd seen it happen at the movies in love stories.

When silence became unbearable again and nothing witty came to my mind, I asked her if she was studying at the Theater Academy. She said she wasn't, but knew an actor, George Paradi, who was going to help her. I knew who he was, but I didn't know at that time that George was the most notorious womanizer in Budapest, surpassing even my brother. When I moved to Montreal, I heard Paradi was jailed in the sixties for seducing two underage girls and taping their voices in the process.

I can't imagine how I mustered enough courage to ask her for a date. She agreed without hesitation. I couldn't believe my good fortune. I suggested we meet the coming Wednesday at six under the clock by the National Theater.

The big clock at the National, on the corner of Rakoczy Boulevard and Grand Circle Boulevard, was the most famous and popular rendezvous spot in Budapest. A song was even written about it before the First World War, and it became one of the most popular hits in Hungary.

When the music stopped we walked back to Suzi's table, holding hands. I thanked her politely for the dance and smiled conspiratorially instead of reiterating our date in front of her friends who were also settling back into their seats.

I rushed back to our box to tell it all to Irvin: the date I'd arranged with Suzi; how she'd rubbed against me during our dance and how she'd fallen in love with me. He didn't believe a word of it. I pleaded with him for the rest of the afternoon but he remained skeptical about my conquest.

I was so taken by my instant success that I didn't want to spoil it by asking anyone else for a dance, or by going back to Suzi to ask her again; I didn't want to jinx my good fortune. Irvin and I just sat in our box until seven o'clock, sipping our drinks, arguing about my conquest and waiting for the dance to terminate.

Monday morning in school, a shy, embarrassed Irvin approached me during the recess after our first class and told me his mother didn't want us to meet so often. She thought I was a bad influence on him. I was not hurt but surprised at her shortsightedness. I believed I was good for Irvin.

After the Saturday dance at the Moulin Rouge I didn't think of Marika for a while. Suzi had taken over my fantasies completely, day and night. I was in love with her. We were to meet in two days but I still couldn't decide where to take her, and if she was willing, where to make love to her, and how to get money out of my parents for the date. I couldn't expect my brother to finance all my adventures.

Followed by hours of agonizing, I decided to take her to the eight o'clock showing of *Citizen Kane*, stopping for a quick espresso before the film if we got there early. Afterwards we could go strolling on Margit Island. There is a small island between Buda and Pest, not as small as Ile St. Louis in Paris, but small enough to be on the Danube and large enough to hold a hotel, an open-air theater and an Olympic pool for water sports. It was a haven, and probably still is, for lovers at night. At that time, Hungarian teenagers didn't have access to cars for making out in the back seat or cruising the boulevards in the evenings. For the young it was the streetcars, long walks in public parks, and if you had luck with your date, alfresco on the Island.

It was Tuesday morning, a day before my big date, and I still didn't know how to get money. My parents and my brother refused to give me enough for me to feel secure on an important date. I was desperate. Irvin never had money; his parents weren't well off and I didn't know anybody in class who could lend me some.

Then, I came upon an intriguing but dangerous idea. I felt excited and guilty about it at the same time. Eve must have felt that way before she bit into the forbidden apple.

My father wasn't a collector of art, or books, or anything people normally hoard in their homes. Whatever artwork we displayed in our apartment was bought as an investment or strictly decoration. He was a pragmatic business-man who only invested in solid bets like gold and foreign currency. However, right after the war he impulsively bought a valuable stamp collection and locked it up in a drawer next to some chocolate bonbons my mother received from one of our dinner guests and kept protected from me.

Early Tuesday afternoon, right after lunch while my mother was washing the dishes, I snuck into the bedroom where the keys to all the furniture were kept in a drawer. Flushed with excitement, I picked out the appropriate key, ran into the living room and pulled out some of the albums filled with the beauti-fully arranged sets of foreign stamps. I took out a few Swiss ones, placed them carefully in my wallet, put the albums back, locked the drawer, and sat for a while to calm down. I knew I was doing the wrong thing but I was compelled to do it. My only consolation was that I stole from my parents and not from strang-ers. Deep down I knew it made no difference; theft is theft whether it stays in the family or not. I committed an immoral act in order to satisfy a hedonistic need; I felt miserable about it, but at the same time, the prospect of making love to Suzi the next day alleviated the pain.

There was a small stamp shop on Barros Square, not far from our street. It was run by a bald, middle-aged man with thick glasses that kept slipping down on his nose. His eyes lit up when I showed him the stamps. To my great surprise he didn't ask how I got them but carefully scrutinized the stamps with a magnifying glass. I did have a story in case of possible questions, but he stayed silent during the examination. I knew he was going to try and cheat me but I was ready for a bargaining session. He looked up from the stamps, pushed his glasses back from his nose and offered a sum. It sounded pretty good, but judging from the circumstances I realized the stamps must have been worth four or five times more. I thanked him and was about to leave but he stopped me and offered fifty percent more. I asked three times his original offer. He accepted. I am quite sure he made a good deal for himself. I walked out with a bundle. I had never had so much money in my life. I felt lightheaded and clammy. On my way home I bought a few packages of Camels on the black market and spent the rest of the day planning.

On Wednesday afternoon, dressed in my zoot suit, I decided to take the streetcar rather than walk to the National. It wasn't a very long walk but I was afraid to get there late, and I didn't want to tire myself–I had a long evening ahead of me. Excited by the promise of the evening, but too anxious to sit peacefully on the wooden bench, I stood on the platform thinking that Suzi must have liked me a lot: she had held me tight against her boobs, put her cheek next to mine as lovers do, held my hand and hadn't objected to my erection. She also accepted my invitation without hesitation. She must be in love, too. These thoughts passed through my innocent mind on the way to my first date with the girl I had seduced on the dance floor of the Moulin Rouge.

As soon as I stepped off the number six streetcar in front of the National, the busiest corner in the city, I felt a pang of fear. It was only half past five on the huge clock. It didn't occur to me until I was standing under the clock, holding a red rose in my hand, that she might stand me up. I smelled the rose, which I bought on Barros Square from a Gypsy woman. It still exuded a wonderful scent, full of unimaginable promise, and I felt less anxious.

By six o'clock I knew she would never show up. I began to think clearly. How could I actually believe that Suzi, at least four years older than I, would go out with me on a date? Why should she? She probably goes out with George Paradi who is famous and has lots of money. Why did I embark on this unrealistic adventure whose outcome should have been obvious from the out-set? I didn't have an answer.

Although I was now certain she wouldn't come, I couldn't leave the spot. Hope is such a depressing emotion. In the meantime I watched dozens of young couples meet and kiss under the clock and continue on to their amorous adventures. I stood there with a rose in my hand fantasizing that the *bitch* would arrive out of breath, apologizing profusely. It is amazing. Half an hour ago I was in love with her; by six thirty she had become a bitch.

The sun was dropping rapidly behind the 19th century buildings on the boulevards. But I remained in my spot rationalzing that since I had already waited this long I might as well stay until seven just in case she had misunderstood me and thought that this was our meeting time. This actually meant, if I held to that theory, I needed to wait until seven thirty in case she was late, and women are notoriously late on their dates, I had heard.

At quarter to eight, two hours after I got off the number six, I dumped the rose in a wastebasket and took the streetcar home. I didn't cry but I wanted to. On my way home I got a window seat and began to muse about Marika again, about our adventures, about her lovely face and voice. I missed her. I felt so sorry for myself that I missed my stop and had to jump off the moving streetcar.

Jumping off streetcars was an art in Budapest. You had to learn how to jump gracefully and accurately. It was important that it look relaxed and casual like a dance step, and it was best if you had a cigarette in your mouth. You just leaned back, held yourself with one hand, swung out and let go. You had to land on your right foot first; landing on the left was suicide. One of our classmates ended up losing a leg under the wheels.

When I got home my mother knew instantly that something had gone wrong. She asked why I was home early when I had begged her for money all day to go see a movie. I told her I had changed my mind but I could see she didn't believe me. She didn't press me further and I was grateful for that.

I went to bed early with my favorite book on inorganic chemistry.

* * *

XI.

FRIDAY I AWAKE from a puzzling dream. The first time in my life I have dreamt about being on another planet–I don't know which one–among a strange species. What could have motivated that dream with its nebulous action, unrecognizable characters, and illegible symbolism, I cannot say. But I must think about it more before I forget the details; eventually, I will find its connection to reality. Nothing happens inside our body without some reason–at least, I would like to believe that.

After having my orange juice and cereal with fresh fruit and milk, and watching *Good Morning America* without listening, I call Cass in her office. She can't refuse my call, considering the attention I have given her the past few days. Of course she can. She can do anything she wants.

"Yes, Gabi," comes her voice distorted by the miraculous workings of electronics. It is confident and slightly impatient.

"Are you with a patient, or by yourself?" I ask politely.

'What difference does it make? I'm here, answering your call," she says, somewhat softer–probably the result of the flowers I have been sending her every day. They must have had some effect.

"I want you to come with me to Santa Barbara for the weekend," I say casually as if we have been having an affair for the past six months. There is a prolonged silence at the other end. She didn't say no immediately, I am thinking: it is the flowers undoubtedly. They are man's best friend. They never fail. I should have started this whole adventure by sending her flowers; we would have made love by now.

"Are you there?" I ask softly.

"Yes, I'm still here, thinking." Well, I am in business if she is still thinking. When a woman doesn't say no it means yes, goes the old wives' tale. "All right," she breathes into the phone, "let's get this over with. Pick me up in front of my building at ten tomorrow morning."

"I'll be there," I say enthusiastically.

"Hold it for a moment!" Oh, no! She's changed her goddamn mind. I can't believe it. "Why don't I pick you up instead? I've got your address on file here." She hangs up. I don't like the way she ended the conversation; it sounded like the promise of a charity fuck. Why would she do that–just to get rid of me? She could have handled it differently; she could have told me that if I didn't stop harassing her she would go to the police or something as strong as that. I am sure that would have stopped me. Maybe she is working on a counter plan I don't know about, some kind of trap. That must be the reason she changed her mind and wants to drive me; or, she is afraid I will kidnap her. She will show up tomorrow with two bodyguards and have them beat the daylights out of me. Who knows? This is still the Wild West in many ways. She could cajole me into the bushes, pull a gun, shoot me dead and plead self-defense.

Instead of rejoicing and celebrating the outcome of my scheming, I develop an uneasy feeling after she hangs up. This is not how I anticipated victory. But when does anything in life turn out the way we hope and anticipate? I should be used to it by now.

Nobody ever made love with me in order to drop me, to get rid of me, to end my pursuit. It sounds ridiculous, absurd. I can't accept it. She is not that kind of woman. She is too strong, too gutsy to behave like that. I don't want charity; I need participation in my fantasy, voluntary participation based on the international rules of seduction. I wanted to look forward to that fuck but now I dread it. Maybe I should call it off, tell her I changed my mind: I don't need her any more, I found someone else who is more willing and looks even more like Marika, and is younger. Yes, that will hurt her, all right. She has been pretty nasty to me; why shouldn't I repay some of the hurt she inflicted on me?

I realize I am covered with sweat—my face, under my arms, my crotch, everywhere. I decide to take another shower.

As I am soaping myself down I develop an erection. I adjust the tap to cool the water.

I return to my study, refreshed, and dial my agent. He tells me a Canadian producer in Vancouver is interested in me as well as an Australian producer who starts shooting on location soon; they haven't come back with an offer yet, however. He will call me at the end of the day. These calls don't excite me anymore; they are meaningless. My name is up there with hundreds of other names and the producers will choose the one whose last picture made the most money, or who has already directed a film just like the one they are producing. I am up for at least sixty films a year, perhaps more. If I am lucky I make one every two years. If you haven't directed a recent hit you have to struggle along with hundreds of directors all trying to do the same film. I am developing my own projects with writer friends and trying to peddle them to studios. That is the only way to do the films I want to do.

I decide to call Phoebe. She is at home and in a good mood.

"Why don't you come over? My parents are out exploiting the suckers. I am alone with the maid. I'd rather be with you," she says, much to my delight.

"I'll be over in half an hour," I say, and rush to the bedroom to get dressed. What has happened to me? I have never looked forward this much to seeing Phoebe before. In a few minutes I am in my car driving through Beverly Hills.

The uniformed Mexican maid opens the door and tells me in barely comprehensible English that Phoebe is in her bedroom. I walk through the hallway and then the living-room, which looks like a picture gallery: the walls are covered with lithographs by Chagall, Miro, Picasso. I am wondering if they were bought wholesale.

Phoebe doesn't look too bad. In a week or so her skin will regain its original color. Her nose is still bandaged but the eyes are clear of disintegrating blood. She smiles like an innocent child as I hand her a bouquet of daisies.

"You're sweet, Gabi." I kiss her on the cheek.

"You can kiss me on the lips. I'm not contagious," she says, and puckers her lips. I lean over to kiss her carefully. I don't like the taste of her mouth: it's stale and full of residual medication and probably decayed molecules that ooze out of her tortured flesh. "Don't you like kissing me anymore?" she asks, reading my mind. She must have noticed my subtle recoil.

"I love kissing you but am afraid to hurt you," I lie.

"Don't bullshit me, Gabi. My mouth must taste like a cloaca . . . I forgot." She pushes me away from her face, to my relief. "Why don't you fuck me? I don't need any foreplay. You touch me and I'm off. You must be horny too, aren't you?" I don't answer the question. I pull off her silk, Christian Dior nightgown, kiss and suck on her erect nipples, one after the other, and begin to knead her breasts.

"Take off your pants and get on with it, hurry!" I do as she says. But, when I turn her over on her back so I can mount her comfortably she stops me. "Fuck me from the side! I don't want you to see my face like this when you come." Does she think I am a fourteen-year-old who might get a negative fixation, whose sex life might be ruined for the rest of his life, who will therefore only enjoy fucking the Wicked Witch of the East? "I want you to see my beautiful face in your mind's eye while you're doing it." Her words strike a sensitive point. I instantly lose my erection. "What's the matter with you, for God's sake? Have you been balling someone else lately?"

"I don't know what happened. Maybe you talk too goddamn much," I say, moderately upset. But Phoebe is relentless in her desire. She leans forward and takes me in her mouth. The sensation is overwhelming. In a second I am ready to penetrate her. I turn her over to her favorite side and we begin. I am making love to Marika and Cass alternately and wondering at the same time whom Phoebe is fucking. Selfishly, I am hoping she is making love to me. She comes with a noisy shriek, then there is silence, peace.

"I am starving," I moan, helping her back to a comfortable position. I kiss her forehead.

"Stop kissing my forehead, Gabi! You're not my father. Do you want to stay for lunch?" she asks. Phoebe talks tough but she is a gentle, kind woman. I haven't quite figured out why she puts on that street-smart style.

The maid brings us sandwiches, a glass of milk for Phoebe and a bottle of imported beer for me, and discreetly places the silver tray on Phoebe's small, cluttered desk. As I watch the maid struggle to make room for our lunch I keep wondering why I am always hungry after lovemaking. I guess it is from the sudden protein loss in the metabolism. I should find out from one of my doctor friends. I have always been curious about this phenomenon.

The tuna sandwiches are wonderful. We are both eating fast and talking with full mouths at the risk of choking.

"I've been working on my screenplay feverishly for the past few weeks. It's going to be good, you know," she says earnestly.

"I am sure it'll be good. But don't get too disappointed if the studios turn you down."

"Don't be so fucking negative, Gabi."

"I am not negative. I am realistic."

She laughs out loud.

"You, realistic? That's a laugh. You're the most unrealistic person in Beverly Hills, and you know the mentality of the population here."

I don't know how to react. How does she know? Is her perception so keen? Maybe she does have talent as a writer, after all. I must read her script.

"I can't wait to read your script. And forgive me . . . I am just protecting you from disappointments," I say with lots of empathy.

"I don't need protection, Gabi. I need help to set it up. I'm sure it's good. It's about real things, real conflicts, real characters."

"That's exactly why I am afraid. Realism is a dirty word in Hollywood. Also, this town doesn't like to embrace filmmakers who don't go through a tremendous struggle and demonstrate to the community that they will persevere against all odds."

"I don't mind the struggle as long as we do the film. It'll help us both. You need a good film; you've done a lot of shit lately." I am listening to her in admiration. Her faith and energy is contagious. "In a few days I'll show it to you. By then I'll be able to show you my new nose as well."

"What will you do if you don't like your new nose?"

"I'll sue the shit out of the plastic surgeon. I had him sign a picture with my future nose outlined on it."

"Let me see the picture!"

"No, it's in my safe. You needn't see it. I want you to get a good, fresh first impression. You'll like it."

On my way home from Phoebe's lunch I try to plan out the rest of the day. It makes me unhappy that I have to think about it; I should be making movies and be less preoccupied with myself. But I can't help it; the strike still lingers on.

At home there are a few messages waiting for me on my answering machine. I think at once that Cass has changed her mind and canceled our trip to Santa Barbara. I can see her doing such a thing. I have to wipe her out of my mind. One day, science will be able to help the pathologically obsessive. I need microsurgery on my brain, a subtle laser lobotomy to erase unwanted images, to short-circuit the projector in my mind.

There is a message from American Express. I owe them some money. They will have to wait until the strike is over. Had I been at home, I would have hung up as soon as I'd heard the automated voice. It is not only annoying but humiliating to talk to a computer. If you owe them money they want to disgrace you, they want to imply you are a nobody, not worth talking to. Let the computer handle those nonentities, they must be thinking.

The other call is from Ben Schtreiber, a writer friend. I relax. Cass has not called off our date after all.

Ben's message asks me to call him back immediately. What can be so urgent? I am working on a project with him but it is not at a stage where I expect emergency calls. Well, I should call him. I am not in the mood for a business conversation but I am conscientious about returning calls. Returning and avoiding phone calls in Hollywood is a subtle art and a pretentious game. When your agent or a studio executive doesn't call you back until seven in the evening you can be sure you were one of the last calls on the sheet. This tells you what they think of you: your importance is in direct proportion to the time elapsed between your call and the response—if it is returned at all.

"Just came back from my new agent," says Ben, sounding as if he just swallowed an apple and it is half way down his esophagus. His voice is normally weak, but this time I can hardly hear him.

"What happened to you? I don't hear you too well," I shout into the receiver as if I don't know it is his voice and not a bad connection.

"Something happened this afternoon that you won't like," he says, his voice raised but hoarse from the effort and emotion. My heart sinks. I know instantly what has occurred.

A few months ago, Boris Doffy, a writer friend, introduced me to Ben at a lunch at Café Roma. Boris is a witty but obnoxious conversationalist who does a good imitation of my Hungarian accent, à la Bela Lugosi. Ben, a short man with a barrel chest and a large head, was quiet at our first lunch and all our subsequent lunches. He would listen, sometimes commenting with a broken sentence or else telling a story at the end of the lunch, which he repeated again and again at every lunch thereafter.

But it was not his silence that bothered me. It was the expression in his eyes; they exuded weakness. At one point, I thought his height might be responsible for his timidity and lack of self-confidence.

After one of our ritual lunches, Ben said he liked my ideas about movies and would like me to read one of his scripts. I was delighted. I am always on the lookout for new material and Boris had praised his work.

I eagerly read the script that same evening and I loved it. I told him it was one of the best things I had read lately (a typical Hollywood parlance that nobody takes seriously anymore) but that it was too long. Ben agreed and asked me if I had any ideas about how to get rid of sixty pages. I said I would try. He then suggested we become partners and co-produce the film, with me as the director. He also suggested that I draft an agreement outlining our relationship because he was not good at writing legal mumbo-jumbo. I still don't know why he assumed that I was good at it.

I spent long hours at night making cuts in the screenplay. He kept saying at our meetings how well I understood his script and that we would make a great film. When I finished the editing job I gave a copy to my agent who loved it and sent it out to some studios. In the meantime, I showed the draft agreement to Ben who said that as far as he was concerned it looked fine but that before signing it he wanted to show it to a friend who knew more about contracts. I said fine, but the little voice, my instinct, sounded an alarm.

During the process of editing and rewriting we had become friends, and I said to myself that not everyone is a con artist in this town. Especially not writers, who are, at best, the conscience of mankind.

But when I heard him say, "something happened," I knew that he'd betrayed me.

"My new agent threatened me that if I signed the agreement you wrote he wouldn't take me on as a client. He wants to send the script out without a director attached, wants to package it in his agency. Believe me, I feel rotten and guilty about this. I didn't sleep last night at all, you must understand. I need a good agent badly. I hated my previous agent; she didn't do anything for me."

The blood rushes to my head; I know I am losing my cool.

"How can you be such a shit, such a weak jerk to cave in to your fucking, pretentious agent? Why didn't you tell him the script comes with me and that's the deal? You have a moral obligation to me!" By now I am screaming.

"I told him, but he didn't want to sign me up if you were attached to the project," he whines.

"Ben, I always expect to be fucked by producers so I protect myself as much as I can, but not by writers. I trusted you because you were a writer. You betrayed me, you little shit." I slam down the phone and pour myself a stiff drink. I am shaking. I wonder what Boris will have to say to this. I return to the phone and call him.

"Your friend Ben just called me," I announce, and tell him the story. Without missing a beat he says, "Well, don't be surprised. Hollywood makes people crazy. He was kicked around for twenty years; he's insecure; he wanted a new, powerful agent. What do you expect of people? Writers are no better than anyone else."

I can't believe what I am hearing. Maybe he is right: this town drives you mad, makes you inhuman, a liar; it makes you betray your friends; it destroys your soul. The sad part is that after a while we don't even notice, or attribute much significance to it.

The news from Ben thoroughly ruins the anticipation of my weekend with Cass. His screenplay was one of the best I'd had for a long time. I'd worked hard on it and lost it. And now I would also have to face the embarrassment when my agent withdrew the project from the studios.

I am too upset to read or work. I check the newspaper for some movies I might want to see. I crave a good European film. There is nothing I really look forward to seeing these days, unlike in the sixties and seventies when you had Fellini, Antonioni, Bergman, Truffaut. Their films were cultural events for me;

I went to see them the day they opened and sat through them twice. These days I hardly see a film that I would mind missing.

I come across an old Carlos Saura film, a remake of *Carmen* as a ballet. I decide to go. The music, at least, will distract me from my problems. I like ballet–perfect subject for the cinema. My very first film, a documentary, was about a ballerina.

I don't mind seeing movies alone. I don't need to share the experience. In fact, when I am in a lousy state of mind, I would rather go alone and sulk without subjecting my friends to my mood.

The film is playing at the Laemmle repertory on Santa Monica Boulevard, one of the art houses in Los Angeles. The theater is tacky but it shows good films. At this hour there won't be many people in the audience, so I will be able to sit in the middle-center, the best place to watch a movie.

The movie is exhilarating. The dancers are great and so is the concept. I enjoy the afternoon and do not even think about my aborted project or about Cass.

At five minutes to ten, I am already downstairs waiting for the BMW to drive into the courtyard, signaling the beginning of the realization of my forty-year-old dream. I am positive she will be late, if she comes at all.

I had a restless night. It is not surprising. I was expecting nightmares and cold sweat, but it didn't happen; I simply didn't sleep well. I can't even recall my dreams. I woke up at three in the morning and went into my study to read Toynbee's *A Study of History,* hoping it would put me to sleep. It didn't. In fact, I got so absorbed in the book that I was still reading it at five. Then I decided to drink some hot milk. That helped. At eight the alarm clock woke me. I did my morning exercises and had a hot shower.

At ten fifteen, Cass arrives without apologies. I find this attitude rather impolite and coarse, unlike her. Perhaps she wants to set a mood; it is part of the trap she is setting for me for the weekend. Or, did she just want to be elegantly late, as would a lady of her social standing? I throw my overnight bag on the back seat of the car and get in next to her.

It has been said that Santa Barbara is the Cote d'Azur of California, home of the rich and fashionable. I don't know Santa Barbara well. I have spent a few weekends there on a ranch overlooking the Pacific, playing tennis and eating well. Occasionally a former girlfriend and I would take long walks in the pretty streets with their Spanish-styled villas and well-tended gardens. I loved that. The city felt peaceful and secure.

Apart from a polite greeting, a few clichéd observations about the weather and some questions about the inn at the ranch, Cass is quiet and pensive as we move along the freeway. I also sense that she is nervous and tense. She definitely is not behaving like a woman eagerly anticipating the consummation of a budding romance. Of course, she never saw it as a romance. Then why did she agree to spend the weekend with me? I should be asking her, not myself, this question. I will when the right moment presents itself. For the time being I am fighting an impulse to talk because I am not sure what to say. The situation is too delicate for small talk and too explosive for the truth.

As I watch the landscape hypnotically zip by, my head drops and I come to. I realize I fell asleep for a second. But was it a second? Did she notice I fell asleep?

"You didn't sleep much last night, did you?" she asks without taking her eyes off the road. Oh, my God! She knows. Did I snore, I wonder? She won't bring that up, I am sure.

"I read late into the night. I am sorry," I say sadly. What is happening here? I must do something to change this stifling mood. "My impression was you didn't want to talk. You look self- absorbed, if I may comment on your mood."

"I don't feel like talking. You may go back to sleep. I don't mind it at all."

"I am fine now, thank you," I say.

I suddenly realize the weather has changed. The Santa Ana has stopped blowing, the heat wave is over. It is a beautiful California day: temperature in the mid-seventies, humidity sixty percent and the skies blue. Why didn't I notice the change in the morning? I should be nervous about this trip but I am not; the perfect weather must be having a calming effect on me. I feel a serenity that I rarely experience these days. Only good things will happen to me from now on, both emotionally and professionally, I believe. I am elated. Why do I feel this way? There is no reason other than the weather and the hope of making love with Cass. I shouldn't think about that. I am on my way to victory but at the moment she is sulking. Perhaps she changed her mind and is afraid to tell me. But she is not the type who would be afraid of anything. I am confused by the conflicting messages.

The two-hour drive seems an eternity. I should start thinking about a story for a film script. All right. So, what do studios want these days? They want *high concept* stories, meaning that you have to be able to express the premise of a story in one exciting sentence. It is always a combination of two incongruous ideas. So, what if an alien drops to earth from a hostile planet. It should be a woman, so she can breed. She looks exactly like a human, like Cass? She meets . . .

"Gabi?" I hear, and wake up. I fell asleep again. "You must be really tired," she says with a slight smile. This time she looks at me. "How do we get to the ranch from here?" she asks. Her vile mood is gone; it is the old Cass again. I give her directions to the inn and we begin to make light conversation.

It crosses my mind as we are checking in that she will insist on separate rooms, but she doesn't. I feel good about the way things have begun to move. I even permit myself some degree of optimism for the weekend. This morning it looked as if the trip would turn into a major fiasco. Not so now.

The inn is rustic, furnished with imitation American antiques, tasteful and clean. It is like a luxurious farmhouse out of *Architectural Digest.*

The moment the bellboy leaves, pocketing my generous tip, Cass suggests that I wait for her in the dining room while she freshens up a bit for lunch. I wash my hands and face with cold water and leave her in the room. On my way down the corridor I hear her putting the safety chain on the door.

The maitre d' stops me at the door, checks my name on the reservation sheet, smiles without wanting to and leads me to a corner table across the nearly full dining room, passing guests lined up with their plates at the buffet table before a spread lavish enough to please Henry VIII.

I have been waiting for twenty minutes by now, have read the dinner menu a dozen times and memorized it for the evening. I have analyzed most of the patrons' likely professions and relationships with their partners. I should have brought along a magazine.

At one o'clock she appears in the doorway with a broad smile, catches my eyes immediately and marches by the maitre d' toward my table. Upon seeing her, my lungs collapse and my stomach shrinks to the size of a golf ball. Am I seeing right? Is this Cass? As I rise from my seat, I take a better look at her: she is in white, but this time she wears a pants suit with a tie and an Indiana Jones white hat. She looks like her twin brother.

I help her with the chair, like a fine gentleman, and we both sit down. She is still smiling.

"I was hoping you'd change into something seductive, like a flowing or clinging silk dress," I say in desperation, and regret it immediately.

"Why should I want to seduce you, Gabi? You're already seduced." She looks around the dining room, presumably for the queue at the serving table. "Shall we?" she asks, and proceeds to Lucullus's table to join the line of the starving, but affluent guests. I follow her close behind and notice she has changed her perfume or deodorant. She smells like those California guys who drive Corvettes with a blonde in the passenger seat. Why is she doing this to me? What a stupid question. She is doing it because she knows I want her and need her desperately. She is taking advantage of me, of my agony.

I am not planning to eat a banquet-size lunch. I take food only from the serving bowls close to me. It is impossible to decide what to pick out of the hundreds of choices. I hate brunches. The rich display of food paralyzes my senses, confuses me; I lose my appetite by the time I have filled my plate. In complete disgust I pick a few items and return to our table by myself. Cass is still at the buffet shoveling a mass of food on her plate. The demonic smile is still on her face. I ask the waiter for a double scotch on the rocks. I need to calm down. Where is it all leading, I ask myself?

"Isn't this a great invention? All that food to choose from. We're so privileged, aren't we?" She says without conviction while balancing a piece of smoked salmon with capers on her fork. I begin concentrating on the capers. Is she going to be able to balance them, or will they roll off the salmon before they reach her mouth? At the last moment, one of the capers falls on the table and bounces onto the floor. She pretends to ignore it. Then another little caper drops out of her mouth just before she can close it. It lands on the table next to her plate. Without showing any annoyance, she quickly picks it up with her manicured fingers and throws it into her mouth.

As soon as we leave the restaurant I realize I am still hungry.

"Do you want to go for a walk, to explore a little?" she asks before we reach the staircase. She ate too much for lovemaking anyway. It is better to take a walk.

We have the whole night ahead of us–why rush? I've waited for decades; I can wait a few more hours.

"Yes, why don't we? Let's walk down to the shore," I say, without much enthusiasm.

"Don't you like walking?"

"Not on an empty stomach," I say innocently. She laughs.

"I noticed you hardly ate anything. Didn't you like the food? I thought it was delicious. I meant to tell you this place was a good choice. I like it here."

Every decent-sized town along the Pacific coast, in and around Los Angeles, has a pier, and Santa Barbara's is lined with gift shops, fast-food stands and a couple of seafood restaurants. I never clearly understood the function of a pier; I don't see the difference between walking along the beach, which I like, or on the pier. Perhaps it is built for fishing, a sport I never practiced.

Cass doesn't mind walking on the pier. She disinterestedly examines seashells and some garish works of art created from the remains of sea creatures. In the meantime, the smell of oil from the fast-food places mixed with rotting fish fed to the seagulls makes me nauseated. I turn around to catch the sea breeze but I cannot find it. I remember that the Santa Ana is not blowing anymore, but there should be some wind from the west. I take Cass's hand and lead her toward the railing. I begin to feel much better, except that her hand is ice cold. This strikes me as odd because it is the middle of the day.

"Are you well?" I ask, genuinely concerned. I should have asked: Are you sick? Why didn't I? "Your hand is cold, and you look pale."

"Really?" She says and disengages her hand. She lifts it to her face to check the temperature.

"It is cold. You're right. I wonder why?"

I want to sit down. I feel slightly dizzy and tired. I look around for a bench but I see none. Perhaps the railing would do. I lean against it, hoping the old, corroded wood is strong enough to support my tired frame. Of course it will. Stupid thoughts. Suddenly, I realize what is happening: I am fighting a premonition.

Tourists pass by, dressed in sloppy shorts or jeans, snapping pictures of the obvious with their Kodaks.

"Have you had enough?" I ask Cass, meaning our walk.

"Enough of what?" Does she really not know, or is she deliberately alluding to the whole affair? I think she'd be happy to provoke me into a fight. Yes, that's what she wants.

"Why don't we go back to the inn and rest for a while?," I suggest, trying to be crafty. I must push her, otherwise, it is not going to happen. I feel better now, determined to be aggressive again.

"Gabi, you sound like a teenager on his first date. Calm down. Before we return to the inn you and I will have to talk," she says condescendingly.

Talk? What the hell does she want to talk about at this point? Did she change her mind? We are booked into a room with a queen-size bed and now she wants to have a *talk* with me, for God's sakes. I am not even sure I want to fuck her anymore. Maybe once and that's it, off my mind and I never want to see her again. As we walk by the famous Biltmore Hotel she suggests we have a drink before heading back to the ranch.

The waiter brings lemonade for me and a champagne cocktail for Cass. She nearly empties the glass in one long gulp, leans back in her chair and closes her eyes. She is beautiful, looks exactly like Marika–miraculous.

"You are not going to like what I have to tell you, Gabi . . .

"How do you know?" I interrupt her.

"Let me talk!" she says with her eyes still closed. "It seems to me that you don't want to get my messages. You believe that your romantic notions and behavior will seduce me. I don't deny that they have some effect on me, but my resistance stems from a very different, much deeper source than you can imagine." I take advantage of her short pause to examine what she just said: A deeper source. What does she mean? Is she an anti-Semite who can't imagine loving a Jew? "I'll be honest with you because you've been open with me. I feel, I owe it to you." She reaches for her glass and empties it this time.

I am experiencing weightlessness. She sounds like an executioner in a totalitarian regime, who convinces you of your guilt despite your innocence and while you are nodding your head in agreement, chops your head off.

She leans back in her chair, presumably for physical support. To emphasize her final statement, she closes her eyes again. She takes an interminable pause. I am beginning to think she has fallen asleep when she starts to speak.

"I suffer from a congenital affliction that is irreversible. I have learned to live with it over the years. Perhaps that is one of the reasons I became a psychiatrist." She stops for a moment to think, then looks up at me. "But I am not sure you'd be able to cope with the problem." My God, the poor woman is dying from some horrible disease and I am ruthlessly, selfishly trying to fuck her. How horrible. "I was trying hard to discourage you but you didn't want to take the hints. Actually, I do like you and am ready to make love with you, but before we return to the hotel you must be aware of my problem. It may generate a negative response in you." She stops and waits, scrutinizing my face. Do I look alarmed, or horrified? What could be wrong with her? Is she one half of Siamese twins with a hideous scar running down her side? "Well, are you ready for the revelation?"

"I am not, but go ahead anyway," I say with a trembling voice.

"I am a hermaphrodite, Gabi," she declares with a cool voice, as if it were the most natural thing in the world. She stares straight into my eyes to gauge my reaction.

I attempt to be shocked but it doesn't work. I can't fake it. I laugh. First slowly, then with the force and progress of an avalanche, I begin to laugh like a maniac. She doesn't quite know how to react, whether to laugh with me, or to be insulted by my outburst. Before I completely calm down, I rise from my seat and lean across the table, close to her face. "I am really, really sorry for you, Cass," I whisper.

The moment I collide with a baby carriage, nearly turning it over to the horror of the uniformed nanny, I realize that I have been wondering like a sleepwalker for hours, along the Main Street, aimlessly endangering pedestrians and myself.

I must pull myself together, calm down and go over it rationally. It is not a tragedy—not for me, it isn't; but what about Cass? I am too selfish about this whole affair. This poor woman must have gone through hell in her life trying to cope with male and female genitalia. It is remarkable, in fact, how well she carries her burden.

But my memories and fantasies of Marika are tainted now. I can't think about her without seeing in my mind the genitals of an hermaphrodite. Will I ever be able to dissociate Marika's image from Cass's? I don't know. I fell into a trap–a horrible predicament. I have been waiting for this moment for so long. Cass was the perfect surrogate, and now, she not only prevented my most cherished fantasy from being realized, she also ruined it for the future. Is this revelation going to destroy me–drive me insane?

I return to the Biltmore, the only place I can find a cab, and drive up to the inn to pick up my suitcase. Cass is not in, the concierge tells me–thank God. I run up the staircase instead of waiting for the elevator. I must get out of here fast; I don't want to bump into her.

I avoid glancing at her clothes scattered all over the room as I hastily pack my overnight bag. I breathe through my mouth to avoid smelling the perfumed air.

On my way back on the train to Los Angeles, I try to stop thinking about "it," but it is like telling yourself you don't have a toothache when your bite is painful. Maybe I should get drunk. I won't be able to work in this state of mind. Thank God I am not on a project right now.

I feel a little better once I am at home in my apartment. I love it here. The presence of my books calms me. For me, books are the best cure for mental and spiritual pain, the only worthwhile solace in the world. As I sit at my desk in the library I can feel the wisdom, like a comforting heat, emanating from the pages. This is my temple, this is the place where I feel at peace with myself.

I take a shower, pour myself a glass of port and sit at my desk. I don't even want to see if there are any messages on my answering machine. The heavy wine burns my stomach a little but I don't mind. Actually, it feels good; it heats my body from the inside.

At that moment a question pops into my mind. What if she lied to me? What if she isn't a hermaphrodite, but a clever liar? She is a shrink, she knows my problems, she knows how to fuck around with my head. What if she lied to make me turn away from her? She knows she can turn me off her by calling herself a hermaphrodite. What a perfect move! She not only escapes from my clutches but screws my head up too in revenge. I should drive back to Santa Barbara and insist on seeing her genitals. If she lied to me, I will rape her. The police won't do anything; she booked a hotel room with me. The room is in my name.

But what if she is a hermaphrodite? What if she reveals her double genitalia? The real image will destroy my fantasies and me. Even if she was turned into a woman after birth by a skilled surgeon she won't look normal; she will look freakish and unnatural. I will associate Marika for the rest of my life with the genitals of a hermaphrodite. I can't do this to myself.

I reach for the phone and call Cass at the inn.

"What if you lied to me?" I blurt it out without any introduction.

"Come and see it for yourself," she invites me, dropping the pitch of her voice at least an octave. I can tell she is smiling too. "Perhaps you'd like to fuck a hermaphrodite? It'd be a new and very special experience for you. Would you like to do that?" She sounds like a siren.

"I don't think I am ready for that experience, Cass. And I still don't believe you're telling me the truth."

"There is no reason for me to come up with such an outlandish lie." She stops and I am speechless for the moment, wondering what else to say. "Well, I am here in bed waiting for you. If you don't show, I'll just have to masturbate. Actually, it's quite an experience for me. As you can imagine, I do it with both hands, one for my pussy, one for my dick. Don't you think I am privileged? You probably think that I am a freak. But I always double my pleasure, think about that. So, I am here waiting for you, Gabi. We can have a wonderful time together." She hangs up.

I am sweating. The sick bitch. All shrinks are sick. I can't figure her out. I am going nuts. The lying goddamn cunt. Yet, why would she lie to me? It has to be true. You don't make up things like this as an excuse. But she is different. She is a cunning, sadistic, warped person. She would do anything, short of committing a crime, to torture some innocent victim, to get revenge against nature for making her a freak. My God! She is a doctor; she should be curing diseases, not causing them.

Marika! I cry out. Where are you? What happened to my desire to make love to you? All these years of longing and dreaming gone up in smoke because of the sick act of an evil woman. I can't let this happen to me.

I get dressed swiftly, call downstairs for my car and drive back to Santa Barbara. I speed all the way but luckily don't encounter a highway patrol. I decide I must verify Cass's sex despite the possible danger to my cherished memory of Marika. I have to know the truth.

I make the trip in an hour and a half, record time for me. I rush to the front desk to get the key to the room rather then knocking on the door. I want to barge in and surprise her while she is masturbating.

"I am sorry, sir. Dr. Atwill checked out an hour ago."

"Did she leave any messages for me?"

"No, sir, she didn't."

"Thank you," I say on my way out. I want to avoid the receptionist's gaze. He is probably gloating and laughing behind my back that I didn't get laid by that fabulous- looking blonde.

I drive back to Los Angeles, this time slowly, aimlessly. I don't want to get home soon. I am drained. This woman is a killer. Instead of roses, I should have sent her a letter bomb.

As I get off the freeway at Wilshire Boulevard, I feel my stomach squeezed by invisible hands. Have I gotten an ulcer in the past twelve hours? I wouldn't be surprised. But I don't think it is an ulcer; I know what it is. The ordeal is not over yet.

Like a somnambulist, I am drawn along Wilshire Boulevard, past Santa Monica where I should turn right toward Century Park East, and on to Palm Street. She must be at home laughing at me, basking in her success.

I park my car near the entrance to her condo. The neighborhood is ominously calm. There is not a soul in sight. The dark street is canopied by rows of trees that filter the hard-edged moonlight. Normally, I would walk circumspectly but this time I march fearlessly toward the apartment building and enter the lobby.

I ring all the apartments at the same time in the hope that someone will let me in. In a few seconds the door buzzes open. It alarms me. I suddenly realize I am participating in a horror film that I have created.

In the elevator I recognize again her masculine deodorant. I feel the rage I experienced in Santa Barbara slowly rising in me as I step out of the elevator and walk down the corridor towards her apartment.

I gently knock on the door but no one answers. I wait for a while and repeat the knock a little louder—nothing. I wait and wait. Nothing. The hand begins to squeeze my stomach again making me double up. I can't give into this pain, I have to fight it. I let my rage take over. With my fist clenched I bang on the door a few times—I feel a little better. There is no answer.

"Cass, are you in there?" I yell in a stage whisper, but there is no answer from inside. "Stop playing games and let me in, please!" I keep yelling in a low and desperate voice. What is she doing to me? What is her plan? What does she expect me to do? Does she want me to break down her door so she can call the cops?

I begin to bang hard on her door again. "Let me in, for Christ's sake!" I scream in desperation now. Not a word from inside. I wait and wait but nothing happens. I put my ear against the door to see if I can hear music or some noise from the TV. Yes, I do hear some noise—moans, shrieks, short gasps. She is fucking.

Is she putting on an act or is she really doing it with someone? What is the difference? It is obvious she is playing with me. I am glad I don't have a gun. I listen for a while, then I straighten up and get ready to leave when I notice an older man peering at me from behind a chain-length crack in his doorway. I look at him, shrug my shoulders and leave.

By the time I enter my apartment I am so exhausted that I don't even want to listen to my phone messages. I go straight into the bedroom, undress, and lie on my back trying to relax. Slowly, I hypnotize myself to sleep.

* * *

XII.

THE MOULIN ROUGE experience was an important turning point in my adolescence. My friendship with Irvin was broken up by his parents, and I realized the futility of running after girls years older than I. The chances of getting laid by a sixteen-year-old girl at my age were absolutely nil. I longed for a girlfriend of my age or younger but didn't know where to find one. I would just have to wait.

I decided to change schools. I became impatient studying Latin, Hebrew, and Judaism at the Jewish Gymnasium, knowing perfectly well that I had enough of those subjects to become a scientist. With my parents' reluctant consent I enrolled in a public Real-Gymnasium that prepared students for studies in the sciences.

In the spring Marika acquired a steady boyfriend who came every other day after work to pick her up. He was in his twenties, a tall mustached fellow with typical Hungarian features: blonde hair, high cheekbones, and the demeanor of a Tatar warrior.

I still thought about Marika a lot. I couldn't help it. She walked under the window of our common room where I studied every day, on her way out for an evening. Made up, she looked older and more sophisticated than I remembered her. Over the past few years she had evidently grown out of my league. My sorrow was incurable.

On days when I was too restless to study or daydream at home, I visited my brother at his knitting mill. It was a five-minute walk from home, situated in one of the shops in a large, modern apartment building complex on Damjanich Street. He always hired good-looking girls to work for him, not without prurient intent. On my frequent visits I shyly talked to them about their work while fantasizing about how to make sexual advances. They teased me and occasionally flirted with me but I wasn't sophisticated enough in the art of seduction to be taken seriously. Also, I was reticent in the presence of my brother, the lady-killer.

One afternoon—it must have been during the summer vacation because I distinctly remember it was warm, the sun still high on the horizon—I was gazing out at the traffic through the large window of the shop. I was waiting for my mother. She worked there in the afternoons during the busy season to help reduce overhead.

From the courtyard of the apartment complex, a girl of my age rode a bicycle out on the street. She wore a light blue pleated skirt and a white blouse. Her long blonde hair danced in the light breeze as she turned the corner in front of our mill, passing only a few feet in front of me. Her eyes were so intensely blue that I could see their color from where I was watching. At that instant I decided I must meet her, though I didn't have a clue as to how to go about it.

Before the end of the school year one of my classmates became seriously interested in bicycle racing. One day he brought to class his brand new Italian racing bike. Everyone was impressed. It was made of aluminum, painted white and blue, and you could lift it literally with two fingers.

Maybe the colors, or else the sophisticated look of the machine, inspired me to take up biking. In any event, I managed to persuade my father to buy me a fancy racing bike. He rarely refused my pleadings for anything that contributed to my improvement, and he obviously hadn't yet checked his stamp collection.

That schoolmate of mine took me to his club and I officially joined, but not without some trepidation. I still hated organizations and mass events. I started participating in some cross-country races, coming in last or dropping out halfway through the race. It didn't bother me too much. I enjoyed racing but I didn't have enough stamina to sustain the pace. I believed that would come later after some serious training and practice. After all, I was only fifteen years old.

A month after I saw the girl in blue on the bicycle I visited my brother's mill again. This time I brought along my racing bike and parked it outside the shop. I posted myself by the window at the appointed hour and waited. Like clockwork, she biked out of the courtyard, in the same blue skirt, heading in the same direction as last time I watched her.

I followed her for a while on my snazzy bike, coolly holding the handle with only one hand. Then I pulled up next to her as she turned into a wider street with little traffic. She looked even more beautiful at close range.

I told her about my brother's shop in her building and that I had seen her a month ago and wanted to meet her. She gave me a quick sidelong glance and a friendly smile, and said I could accompany her to her piano lesson.

When I said good-bye to her at the apartment building where her piano tutor lived, she agreed to go to a movie with me over the weekend.

I was so thrilled by my easy success that I raced back to the mill and bragged about it to my brother. He immediately knew the girl I was talking about. He approved of my choice, saying, "She is a pretty little thing," and that he saw her often on her bike coming out of the courtyard. Thank God she was too young for him.

Elated by my adventure, I bicycled home. It was the first time in my life I had a real date with a girl who wasn't going to stand me up. I knew she wouldn't. I judged her honest and innocent, and a little shy. I was so thrilled by life, my success, my sudden progress into the realm of adults, that I took both my hands off the handlebar and rode home whistling the *Radeczky March.*

It was a hot, sunny afternoon, like most days during a Hungarian summer. By the time I got upstairs to the second floor, carrying the bike on my shoulder, I was sweating. At the end of the corridor, in front of her apartment, I noticed Marika's stepmother sunbathing in a low beach chair. She wore skimpy shorts and the top of a bathing suit. I said hello as she looked up at me from her romance novel. I could tell from the soft, yellow cover what she was reading.

One of her legs was pulled up so she could rest the book on her knee. Her loose shorts afforded a view of her pink panties. I slowly, deliberately opened the door to our apartment, fumbling with my keys so I could stare at her crotch a few moments longer. She must have noticed my rising excitement for she replied to my greeting with a soft, sexy voice, and invited me for coffee some time when I would be able to get away from my studies. I was going to say why not now, but I was scared, and too preoccupied with the girl in blue. But it also could have been that I felt guilty of soiling my memories of Marika.

I rolled the bike into the hallway and leaned it against the white round table where my father had his breakfast of two soft-boiled eggs every day. I looked at my blue bike—I couldn't find a blue and white one—with admiration, pride, and gratitude.

I went into our common room to my little red desk and opened a textbook. I couldn't concentrate at all. My mind was on Eva, the girl in blue, and our movie date. I tried to figure out which would be the best movie to see, but even more important was the right choice of theater. Some of the old neighborhood cinemas were built with boxes, an ideal place for couples to neck. In school, kids circulated sensational stories about couples being caught screwing in those boxes. Once, according to rumors, the ushers surprised a couple and they got stuck together, couldn't separate themselves. The ambulance had to take them away wrapped in a sheet.

These silly thoughts plagued my mind, as well as the image of Mrs. Toth's pink panties stretched across her pussy *outlining* its shape. She turned me on. I wasn't thinking about Marika much anymore; I had virtually succeeded in putting her out of my mind, or at least, I had reduced the frequency with which her face appeared in my imagination.

Now I was troubled by Mrs. Toth's interference with my fantasies about Eva. I was longing to be with Eva but wanted desperately to see beyond Mrs. Toth's tight, pink panties, to penetrate her right there on the beach chair. I decided to go out to the corridor and stare again at her crotch. After a while she might invite me for a coffee again. I closed my books and stepped outside. She was gone.

There was a great deal of excitement at home about Hungarian politics—a subject I loathed with all my heart but couldn't ignore. My father labored hard for the Communist Party's success in the 1948 elections and, according to him, they had a very good chance. Of course they had a very good chance with the Red Army standing by and the fanatics manipulating the polls.

The Party officials promised him an important job in the business sector once they came to power. The prospect of my father's new career overshadowed everybody else's problems in the family. It was assumed we were all problem-free.

During this difficult period in my life nobody paid any attention to me. Not that they could have helped me but they could have asked the right questions instead of ignoring me. My brother, at least, provided some marginal help since I was more open with him than with my parents.

Reluctantly, I returned to my books and began to work on math and physics. I always started with subjects I liked in case I got tired or distracted and had to stop studying. In principle, I loathed school but loved learning. I was terribly curious about the world, the universe, how everything worked and was put together. Whenever I received a toy as a child I immediately took it apart to see how it functioned, what made it work.

School was torture. I hated most of the kids in class; I wanted to be alone with friends I chose, not with a group of dumb strangers day after day, year after year. For me, the ideal system of learning was tutoring, as in the old days. Unfortunately, I wasn't so privileged and had to put up with the inconveniences of attending school. Oh God! I hated it.

I daydreamed regularly of being an aristocrat and living a useful and noble life in the company of friends, women and books. I hated everything collective; I hated group activities and group sports. I hated Communism with a passion. The first time in my life I started a real argument with my father was about politics and the Party.

Saturday afternoon I walked to Eva's apartment building and calmly waited for her to show up. I knew she would be there. She came down at three o'clock on the dot, dressed in her blue pleated skirt and a pink sweater I hadn't seen before. As I greeted her I noticed that when she smiled, her face assumed an unusual air of maturity. I had never seen a smile like this on a child's face.

On our walk to the Rex Cinema, a neighborhood theater on Istvan Boulevard, I found out she was an orphan being brought up by her uncle. It turned out she was a year older than I. She didn't patronize me, though, perhaps because she was quite shy.

She didn't object at all to the box seats. They were a little more expensive and also there was the risk of having to share the box with another couple. But this was an early afternoon show and fortunately nobody took the two chairs behind us.

They showed a Western with Franchot Tone, a perfect choice when your interest lies elsewhere than the screen. Right after the lights dimmed, I maneuvered myself close to her so that our knees touched; she didn't move away from me. That was a good sign and gave me incentive to continue my subtle approach. It took me a long while to decide on the next move. The wonderful thing about dating in a movie house was that you could always pretend to be watching the film and to be completely absorbed in it; this way your lack of experience with girls wasn't instantly given away.

It took me twenty minutes to muster enough courage to place my right arm around her waist, right on top of the trimming on her sweater. Why was I so slow? Did I want to project a gentlemanly bearing, or was I simply afraid of rejection? In retrospect, I think it was a little bit of both.

Five minutes later, when my arm started to tingle, I moved my hand under the trimming and touched her bare skin. My eyes automatically closed so I could savor the new sensation without the visual interference of the screen. It wasn't that I had never touched female skin before but I had never touched skin under a garment before. I inadvertently discovered one of the principals of eroticism.

She didn't react to my touch at all. I took a quick sideways glance at her: she was watching the film with great concentration. Did she feel my touches at all? I couldn't tell. I knew instinctively that girls were supposed to pretend as if they felt nothing; boys had all the fun. She sat there like a mummy in a sarcophagus tolerating my insecure advances up her side, inch by inch.

Twenty minutes later I arrived at her hairy and sweaty armpit. The new sensation, and my hand's close proximity to her breast, gave me a hard-on. Thank God she wasn't ticklish for I fumbled in her armpit for at least fifteen minutes before I quickly slid my hand over to her right breast and touched her nipple. It felt wonderful for me but she didn't even flinch. I was sure she would object. It was disappointing that she didn't. First, I had wasted almost fifty minutes getting there, when I could have accomplished it in less than a minute; second, she might be more experienced than I thought she was, in which case my love for her would change. It would cease to be a romantic love; it would become instead a sexual interest—which was great, though it confused me that she was so much more experienced than I.

At that point my arm went to sleep completely and I let it drop. It took fifteen minutes before I could lift it again. I sensed that it was foolish to do the same thing again since it would get boring. And my erection was gone by that time.

I figured the next step was to kiss her. I wasn't sure whether I should kiss her cheek or lips first. By the time I decided to start with her cheek, the film had ended and she rose from her seat telling me how much she liked the movie. I took her hand and we walked out of the theater and headed home.

The sun had almost sunk below the horizon by the time we reached her apartment building. With a pain in my groin again I was thinking of kissing her good-bye before going home when she asked if I wanted to come upstairs. Her uncle was out for the evening. I said yes, but couldn't decide if I was happy about it or afraid of her expectations.

She lived on the fifth floor in a relatively small apartment. All I remember is her simple, dimly lit room, and her bed in the far corner. We sat down on the edge of the bed and I didn't have any idea what to do next. Should I kiss her, or talk about school, or ask for a glass of milk, or make love to her? I didn't know how to make love. I thought if she wasn't a virgin she would show me how to do it.

I took a deep breath and kissed her on the mouth. This time she responded and we began chewing on each other's lips. At one point, she leaned back on the bed. I followed her tentatively and ended up next to her on my side. I had a sudden urge to put my hand up her skirt. I thought she had been very accommodating so far—why not try it? I slid my hand carefully up her thigh and encountered no resistance at all. We were still kissing when my hand reached the edge of her panties. My heart started up like a hot-rod. For the first time in my life, I was going to touch a pussy.

In those days panties were not as tight fitting as they are today. My hand reached her pubis without trouble and searched for her vulva. When I touched her she made a sudden noise that was unfamiliar to me. I asked if I hurt her but she just shook her head and continued kissing me passionately. At this moment we heard the turning of a key in the outside door. We jumped up, she straightened her skirt and I dried my fingers on the bed cover.

A tall man wearing thick glasses and the robe of a Catholic priest entered her room. She introduced me to her emaciated-looking uncle. A few minutes later I fled the place. I am still wondering what would have happened if he hadn't shown up–probably not much more.

As I strolled home down Hernad Street I couldn't decide how I felt about Eva. I didn't like her uncle much and I thought it strange that a girl like her would live with a priest. It didn't make sense to me–it was too out of line with what I knew about families. It didn't occur to me then that the poor girl didn't have any other choices available to her. I didn't feel comfortable with the situation but I was aroused by her willingness to play the boyfriend/girlfriend game.

I started sneezing violently. I didn't have a cold; it must have been the precursor to my allergies that later developed with full force. I blew my nose into a handkerchief and noticed a new smell on my hand, exciting and unfamiliar to me. It was obviously Eva's smell. It made me proud. Well, it was happening to me, I thought; I was getting closer and closer to the real thing.

Even in my bed I didn't stop smelling my fingers. As I kept reviewing the day's events I found it hard to fall asleep. I was upset at not having a best friend to brag to about my conquests and to help evaluate the situation. I didn't want to discuss it with my brother because I knew he would have said, "you should have fucked her before her uncle came home."

The next few days I was very busy. My favorite teacher in school had asked me to run the chemistry club the following year and before the new school year started, I had to plan for our program for the entire year. I was thrilled to be doing it; after all, chemistry was my main interest in life besides losing my virginity.

Toward the end of the week I was still laboring on my plans for our club when my parents announced that they were going out with their friends to a restaurant. I didn't pay much attention to this until I saw Marika leave with her boyfriend soon after my parents. I stopped working.

Even before my secret, deep-seated thoughts became conscious, a jolt in my groin shook me up. It was just a question of finding a ruse to barge into Mrs. Toth's apartment. I knew she would take over from there. Soon, I came upon a simple but crafty idea: I was going to ask her for some milk to have with my coffee. It was customary in Hungary to borrow from your neighbors.

I assumed that the word "coffee" would remind her of the invitation I had stupidly turned down days ago. Had I not turned it down, I'm sure by now I would have made love to Eva and could have continued to work on my studies with peace of mind–very hard to achieve at that age.

I knocked gently on her door. I didn't have to wait long. She let me in with a wicked smile and mischief radiating from her charcoal Gypsy eyes. I quickly told her about the milk and coffee to which she reacted exactly the way I had anticipated. She asked me to sit down and have coffee with her there, knowing precisely what I was after. As she put on water for the coffee she went straight to the point.

"Do you have a girlfriend, Gabi?" I told her about Eva while she was fussing with the coffeepot; about seeing a film with her and kissing her. She asked me if that was all we did, emphasizing the word all, giving it the meaning I wanted to hear.

She wore her familiar dressing gown and looked even sexier now that she had my full attention without Marika's distracting presence. I was sure she was naked under the gown.

As we drank our coffee she asked with her innate coquetry if I would know what to do with girls. I blushed, though I did not think it showed on my sun-tanned skin. I told her shyly, gazing into my murky coffee, that I knew the theory but hadn't actually done it yet. She slowly put her cup down on the table without altering her mischievous smile and leaned close to my ear, as if to tell me a secret that she didn't want anyone to overhear.

As she spoke, her hot breath on my cheek and ear gave me goose pimples on my back. She was asking in a stage whisper if I wanted to learn the way with girls. I took a deep breath and told myself: now or never. I lost my voice, so I just nodded my head. She took the cup out of my shaking hand and led me into the messy bedroom.

She left the door to the kitchen slightly ajar, just enough to let some light from the courtyard filter into the curtained bedroom. It created enough illumination so that artificial light, which might inhibit me and reveal some wrinkles on her face or unwanted bulges on her body, was unnecessary.

The unmade beds, the residual scent of women, the female garments strewn all over the furniture, intimidated me. I looked for a chair to sit on but she guided me to the bed. She knew what to do with a shy teenager; I wasn't given time for second thoughts or indecision. Perched on the edge of the bed I waited for the big moment.

Mrs. Toth put her hand on my face and gently stroked it a few times, then ran her fingers through my curly hair. In a whisper, as if instinctively knowing how to preserve the magic spell, she asked me if I had seen a female body in the nude. I told her I had once, but from far away and only from the back—I didn't dare say it was Marika's.

She rose from the bed and stood in front of me, fully enjoying the process of my sentimental education. She ceremoniously undid the belt of her gown and let it drop on the floor with casual ease as if she performed the act nightly in a club. I was right: she was stark naked under the gown. Her body looked as firm and well-shaped as Marika's but it was darker and more dramatic, probably because she stood right in front of me with her black pubis in my eyeline. Her breasts were medium-sized and firm, with prominent, dark areolas, and nipples as large as pacifiers. The shape of her legs was perfect, like a French woman's, emphasized by the high-heeled slippers. She executed a pirouette to show off her well-shaped buttocks and ended up four inches in front of me.

It is remarkable how ordinary women, ones you wouldn't even turn to look at on the street, become sexy and irresistible in the nude. The female body is the greatest reward for the miseries endured on our planet. At fifteen it was a revelation to me.

She asked me to kiss her nipple, offering one of her breasts in her palm like an apple on a golden tray, and instructed me to take it in my mouth, and not to be afraid to touch and stroke her wherever I wanted. I was stunned and so excited I didn't know what to do first; it was like starting on a ten-course Chinese dinner.

I began sucking on her tits automatically, with such vigor as I must have done to my mother's breasts in my first day of existence. In the meantime she unbuttoned my shirt and pants, then placed both my hands on her breasts and asked me if they felt good. I was in such ecstasy that I couldn't answer–I just did what she asked.

She gently pushed me on my back and removed my clothes. I closed my eyes. The sensation of her lips and tongue running up and down on my stomach was so intense, was such a new experience that I kept thinking of never wanting it to end, that she must keep at it, keep me forever floating in a pleasure vacuum. She then took me in her mouth and I burst instantly. She smiled. I kept wondering what she did with the stuff that came out of me.

She lay down next to me and asked if I wanted to see her pussy, well hidden by her bushy, untrimmed pubic hair. I said yes. She sat across from me on the bed, spread her legs and described every detail of her sex organ. Then she took my hand, placed my finger on her clitoris and asked me to rub it gently. She said it was good for her and for the girls I would be seeing in the future. She was an excellent teacher.

Touching her pussy got me excited again. I was more relaxed, enjoying the situation better now. Soon, I felt her hand on my erection. She leaned back on a pillow, opened her legs and placed me inside her. I could hardly breathe. She made me move slowly, then faster until I exploded again with unfamiliar, exhausting pleasure. No wonder the French call orgasm *le petit mort.*

As we lay there she stroked my hair again, telling me how nice it had been, and what a good student I turned out to be. Then it struck me that I never kissed her on the mouth. I wasn't sure why but I didn't want to, perhaps because of her age. She must have sensed it too for she didn't try to kiss me.

When I was ready to leave she kissed me on the cheek and said I could see her for more lessons whenever I wanted. Well, I was fortunate; I didn't have to worry about my next date with Eva, or with others after her.

As I lay awake in my bed at home I reviewed the events of the day step by step. I became so aroused that I was tempted to get up and return to Mrs. Toth's for more. But I didn't. I suddenly felt like an adult; I believed my adolescence was over. For me, at that age, the act of lovemaking was a more logical turning point than the traditional Bar Mitzvah, which is determined by the chronological age, whether one is ready for adulthood or not.

I was proud of myself that night.

After those pleasant thoughts I suddenly realized that I had missed something. Now that I knew what an extraordinary experience lovemaking could be, I felt cheated that I had never made love with Marika, the girl whom I loved more than anybody. This sudden upsurge of love for her came to me with such power that I completely forgot Eva and even Mrs. Toth. I began to project my pleasures with Mrs. Toth to my fantasy fucks with Marika. I kept thinking, I must make love with her even if I have to wait years; one day she has to break up with her boyfriend and by then I'll know what to do. Unfortunately, in those days, she didn't care much about me. She was polite but so preoccupied that she didn't even stop to talk to me. A few months later she married the mustachioed warrior. I wondered if she had been a virgin when we had our Hüvösvölgy experience.

I decided I would have to try harder to forget Marika. She had graduated to another level, as I had, and we would not likely ever come together romantically again.

Yet despite my contrary desires to love her and to stifle her image, she stayed with me over the years, unfulfilled—an obsession I will never be able to rid myself of.

* * *

XIII.

IN MY DREAM, I am back in the Santa Barbara hotel room with Cass wearing only the white suit jacket, just long enough to hide her crotch. Her long legs are bare and I sense that she doesn't have panties on. As she starts slowly unbuttoning her jacket in front of me, I become anxious about the revelation of her sex organs. Then suddenly, her muscles begin to bulge and Cass's body turns into a weight lifter's. She quickly develops superhuman strength and grabs me with iron hands, pulling me onto the bed and forcing me to make love to her. During the struggle I kick her in the groin which causes both her genitals to explode and melt away like a blob in a second-rate science fiction film. At the same time her Schwarzeneggeresque body shrinks into the shape of an adolescent girl. At this moment, she turns into Marika. Nude, she asks me lasciviously to make love to her. I begin kissing her passionately and soon I am ready for love. She spreads her legs to accommodate me, but as I attempt to penetrate her I discover that she has no opening. She keeps begging me to make love to her and I keep thrusting hopelessly into her groin but can't enter. I awake in a cold sweat, with a nasty headache and an erection—a double punishment.

It is early Sunday morning, and the sky has already turned steel blue beyond the Hollywood Hills when I go back to bed. I sleep all day Sunday—waking up twice, once to go to the bathroom and around noon, to drink some milk and chew on some cookies. I need the rest and the sleep—but not the nightmares.

Monday morning, as I drink my coffee at my desk and listen to the news, I make a resolution to give up on Cass, to never call her again. I must forget her; I don't want my memories of Marika soiled by Cass's sick games. I want to cherish Marika's image and my past experiences with her, however frustrating they may have been.

There is good news on the radio this morning: the end of the actors strike, the longest ever in Hollywood, has been announced. Work on TV shows and movies will begin immediately; I'll be too busy to dwell on my past. I must make some money and develop a script that I love, and straighten out my career.

The little red light on my answering machine is still blinking. I haven't listened to my messages yet. There are two calls from my tennis partners about a doubles game, and Phoebe wants me to call her back.

Her voice on the tape fills me with warmth and affection. She is earnest and direct and doesn't play nasty games. Why didn't I pay more attention to her in the past? The reason I haven't taken her seriously is the age difference between us. There is hardly any hope for bringing up a happy family under those circumstances.

I call Phoebe but she is not at home. I am disappointed. I want to talk to her, listen to her raspy voice, and enjoy her cheerful, life-loving, irreverent attitude toward the world. For the first time since I have been seeing Phoebe, I am upset about not getting through to her. Why isn't she at home taking care of her mutilated nose? She's got too much energy to stay in bed, to be sick; she is not the type who feels sorry for herself. I leave a message on her machine to call me and at the end I add something I have never said before: "I miss you."

As soon as I hang up my agent calls. He has set up a meeting with some

TV producers for this morning. I barely have time to shower and dress before I am on my way to Studio City. The San Fernando Valley is hot, normally ten degrees warmer than Century City. I switch on the air-conditioner in the car, though I hate doing it; it makes me sneeze.

My meetings usually go well. The TV industry in Hollywood is civilized and professional. The TV people know their business and have no illusions about the worth of their work: it is unpretentious entertainment and social drama at its best. They are not infiltrated by incompetent hustlers the way the feature film business is. Every horny, small-time crook in town who wants to get laid appoints himself a producer giving a bad name to the profession.

After my routine meeting I call Phoebe again but she is still out. I don't leave any messages this time. On my way to the parking lot at Warners I run into an actor friend who invites me for lunch in the commissary. I am relieved that I don't have to eat alone today; I am still in a foul mood.

He is a decent young fellow, but like most actors, he talks too much about himself and his career. In a way it is endearing to listen to all that youthful enthusiasm; it is contagious.

After lunch, on my way home, I am still thinking about that actor. Was I jealous of his passionate ambition, his energy, and his resolution to act only in worthwhile projects? Yes, I was jealous. He made me feel aged, jaded and cynical. I can't afford to let myself project cynicism. A creative person cannot be cynical—shouldn't be cynical. Perhaps, I am a bit of a misanthrope but that's another matter. There are as many justifiable reasons to hate mankind as to love it. Why should I love Man unconditionally? What has Man done to this world, to his fellows during our short history on the planet to endear himself to me? Not much. He has spread greed and hatred. Scientific and technological developments have helped us to live safer and more comfortable lives than our forefathers did, but at what price? We are drowning in our own waste and garbage. Morally, humans have a long way to go. I am not too optimistic about "progress".

Artists and philosophers have tried and still are trying to improve Man, but mostly without success. Some believe love is the answer to our problems; it does help, but love is too ephemeral. How many friends and women have I loved throughout my life? What happened to them? Where are they now? If we are lucky, we love ourselves; most people don't even enjoy that privilege. So, what do we do in this world? Pursue love? But it rarely lasts. We need to strive for something more permanent. Art? I suppose so. Art and pure science seem the only worthwhile occupations for Man. Creation, re-creation of reality from the artist's point of view. But aren't art and pure science too individualistic, too idiosyncratic and elitist for mankind to live by? We need something more accessible than art and science. What should it be? For some it is faith. But religion is a dangerous territory too; the arguments are well known and too obvious. Still, there is something to be said for faith. Faith in what? Perhaps faith in peaceful coexistence based on classical moral principles; faith in the purpose of existence for its own sake, for the joy of living, of being alive; faith in the purpose of living a civilized life. I am back to love again, that is where the cycle leads me. Faith in love. We must make love work, we must prevent its disintegration, we must work for its permanence.

As I drive along Wilshire Boulevard heading home I pass Cass's medical building. I could have taken a different route to Century City but an unconscious, indescribable power guides me in this direction. Upon reflection, perhaps it is not so unconscious and less powerful than I try to represent it to myself.

Like a sleepwalker who doesn't have the power to alter the drive of his subconscious, I automatically slam on the brakes and park in front of her office building–illegally. I dash into the lobby, and squeeze into a crowded elevator at the last second, just before the doors close.

I barge into Cass's office. The astonished secretary tries stopping me but I push her aside rudely and enter the inner sanctum.

Cass is at her desk working on papers as I throw open the door. She looks up and waves away her secretary, who by now has caught up with me in the doorway. She closes the door behind me with an expression of deep disgust frozen on her face.

I am alone with Cass again. She keeps looking at me without a word, waiting for my gambit to start the conversation, I assume.

Confronting her again suddenly paralyzes my thought processes. I don't know what to say to her that is new and revealing and convincing, that would help reestablish a relationship meant to be romantic but become a contentious nightmare.

"I want you to forgive me for being a nuisance and a complete jerk. I had to do it," I say, to my great surprise, still slightly out of breath.

She leans back on her chair, and sighs with relief, I presume, that I didn't produce a knife or a gun but instead apologized and behaved like a gentleman.

"I understand," she says without much conviction and takes her time to add, "but I don't approve of your behavior. There are better ways to attempt to cure your neuroses, Mr. Fodor . . ."

I am stunned for a moment hearing my surname.

"But I am cured, I have to admit. You tainted my cherished fantasies with your loathsome games and ruined them for me. I'll never see Marika in my mind as pure and innocent as I did before. You stigmatized my memories of her."

"Don't blame me for your actions, Mr. Fodor. I didn't initiate your therapy. You came to see me with a problem and I tried my best to discourage you and help you at the same time."

"So, what you're saying is that your sexual affliction is not for real, you just used the idea to drive me insane," I scream, losing my cool again.

"Calm down, calm down. You have no right to ask me any more questions. True or not is not an issue here anymore. You just told me you're cured. And I also believe you're cured. So, please, go home and relax. The therapy has worked." She rises and extends her hand. I have no choice but to take it.

On my way out of her office I stop in the doorway for a second to take a last look at her. I realize suddenly she doesn't quite look like Marika. She looks like most of our TV stars: blonde, cold and artificial.

After lunch I reach Phoebe. She is out of breath from running to answer the phone.

"We just came in from the hearing. Dad is furious at the judge. He put the jerk on a six-month probation and assigned him to some community work, big deal. He got off Scot-free, the little fuck. But I've prepared a lovely surprise for him, you'll see. I am organizing a nose- unveiling party Saturday and I want you to come, of course. I am also inviting the jerk . . ."

"How can you do that after all . . ."

"Don't get excited, Gabi. It's part of my scheme, you'll find out. Someone's got to punish him for my suffering."

"Are you taking the law in your own hands?" I ask half- seriously.

"Don't be an asshole, Gabi. I am not going to let this little shit get away with murder."

"Well, it's not exactly murder, and he is punished . . . "

"You call wrapping turkey sandwiches for the homeless punishment? You must be joking. But that's enough on the subject. By the weekend, I'll have another surprise for you . . . "

"I've had one too many lately. I am not sure I am ready for another. What is it?"

"I finished my screenplay. I am going to shut you up in my room until you finish reading it in one sitting, the way a script should be read."

"Am I going to see you before the weekend?" I ask her casually, trying to maintain my old attitude toward her.

"That's unlike you, Gabi. What's happening to you? Are you mellowing? You used to call me half-an-hour before you needed a fuck . . . "

"You're exaggerating, Phoebe. It sounds funny, all right, but I don't think it's the case."

"You do sound different, though," she says.

"Well, yes, or no?"

"I want to surprise you Saturday, and I need the time to type out the script. I'll see you at three o'clock. It's going to be a garden party."

I am disappointed but I have no choice. Now that the strike is over I need some time to myself to prepare projects and to meet producers and studio executives. I will be distracted for the rest of the week, anyway. Also, I need the solitude to reflect on my past and my future, both emotional and professional. I think they are more interwoven than I ever believed. They seem to rise and fall at the same time.

By the time I arrive at Phoebe's house Saturday afternoon there is no parking left on the street; I give my Porsche to the Mexican valet.

It is a mixed crowd of students and friends of Phoebe's family, and I can spot a few of her teachers I know from USC.

Maids in black and white uniforms snake among the guests offering canapés on silver trays, and a young African American butler, probably an out-of-work actor, supplies champagne to the lively crowd. Phoebe is nowhere to be seen. I sense a certain expectation in the air.

On my way to the pool area I greet Phoebe's parents. They are pleased to see me; I don't know why. She may have told them I am one of her professors. I eat a few of the unidentifiable petits fours and quickly wash them down with a glass of good California bubbly before their true taste can register on my taste buds.

Across from the pool, to my surprise, I notice the punk talking to some kids from USC. He's got nerve. He is laughing and doesn't give the impression that he has been at all cowed by our punitive system. He is having a wonderful time. I don't understand why Phoebe's parents agreed to his presence at the party. They must be in on the punishment Phoebe has devised for him.

I am anxiously waiting for Phoebe to show. I have been longing for her all week, trying to imagine what she will look like with her new nose. I hope they didn't ruin her look. What if I hate her new face? Am I going to say, "Your face doesn't look good anymore, Phoebe. I don't think I want to see you anymore." I doubt that I will insult her; after all, she is a wonderful girl and smarter than most women I have met.

I haven't been a serious partygoer since my bachelor days and I don't consider myself single now. I enjoy Phoebe and I want this relationship to develop into something deeper, though I didn't intend it initially. Parties are only fun when you are on the prowl.

At the far end of the garden a small tent has been erected to house the buffet which will open up after the unveiling of princess Phoebe. I am hungry but cannot eat any more of the food, which disgusts me. Perhaps another glass of champagne? Why not? I need it.

From where I stand I can see two girls of Phoebe's age pick up an antique armchair and carry it across the living room into the hallway. What's going on? Where is Phoebe? She certainly knows how to build suspense. Maybe her script is going to be good. Oh, yes, I almost forgot. She wants to lock me up in her room this afternoon to read her script. But right now, I have no idea where she is. She could have escaped from the party. The operation didn't make her look good, she hated her new nose and left before the guests could comment on the job. They screwed up her unique face. I am sure that is what happened, otherwise she would be here showing off her new identity.

Two young men in white dinner jackets appear in the doorway between the garden and the living room. They hold trumpets at their sides, waiting for a cue. I notice Phoebe's mother in her new white Chanel dress cross over to the young men, say something to them and then leave.

I think it is time for me to find someone to talk to. I am tired of second-guessing Phoebe's scenario for the party. As I am moving off, suddenly the two young trumpeters blow a royal fanfare. Conversation stops and everyone turns toward the main door to the house.

Four girls dressed in white carry a makeshift litter converted from the antique armchair. Phoebe sits proudly in it. She is dressed in a flimsy sky-blue silk dress with a matching veil covering her face. The crowd cheers and applauds this preposterous manifestation of a Beverly Hills party theme.

I am surprised Phoebe has gone along with her mother's idea for a theme party. On the other hand, it could have been her idea—who knows? Perhaps she wanted to amuse me, make this a send up of theme parties. That makes sense to me. She has a wicked sense of humor.

The girls lower the litter near the pool and the two young men blow another fanfare. The crowd moves closer to have a better view of Phoebe's new nose. Her parents seem anxious; I can detect a slight embarrassment in her father's behavior as he tries hard to be amused by it all—he must have had a different upbringing.

Phoebe gracefully steps out of the litter and whispers something to the girls who carried her out. Their searching eyes stop on me. What did she say to them about me? Two of the girls approach me in a hurry. The guests watch in silence and anticipation, which makes me nervous. I don't like to be put on the spot. I look behind me to see if they could possibly be going toward someone else.

As they reach me, each takes an arm and sweetly asks me to follow them. I can't resist their invitation, nor can I insult Phoebe, whatever her design may be. As we reach the litter I realize what Phoebe wants me to do. I am touched by her thoughtfulness.

As we arrive at her side, the live band on the other side of the pool starts to play, "For she's a jolly good fellow . . . " The guests join in the chanting, "Phoebe is a jolly good fellow . . . !"

When I hear Phoebe say,

"Do it, Gabi!" I step in front of her and with both hands, like a magician about to reveal the vanished head of his assistant, I lift her veil. The crowd applauds and cheers, and the band continues to play, "Phoebe is a jolly good fellow . . . "

"How do you like it, Gabi?" she asks, smiling at me and at the cheering crowd. I take her arm and lead her away from the litter and the girls, walking with her amidst the applauding guests as if we were newlyweds.

"You looked stunning before, and you look breathtaking now. In fact, I want to make love to you right now."

"First, I have some business to attend to and then you'll read the script." She kisses me and strides off. People go up to her, congratulating, kissing and admiring her as she winds her way through the celebration.

I stand where she left me, watching. She goes up to the punk who is in the middle of a small group of students, takes his hand and walks him towards the pool, right up to the edge. She smiles at him, I can see her well, and clenches her right fist.

It happens with lightning speed: like an expert fighter, she throws a fast and powerful punch right smack into his nose. The unexpected impact throws him off balance and into the pool. The crowd instantly quiets. Her father and I run over to her side in case she needs protection. The punk is struggling to swim in his loose clothes, a red path streaking behind him in the clean water.

"He bloodied up the water, the little bastard. I hope he doesn't have AIDS, we just had the pool cleaned," says her mother in disgust, and joins the little group at the poolside. I am watching Phoebe's smile of fulfillment and the crowd's reaction; they are expecting a third act, I presume.

The punk climbs out of the pool and looks around, touches his bleeding nose. Phoebe's father approaches him with two male guests at his side.

"Now, get the hell out of here, you son of a bitch or I'll give you another one you won't forget," hisses Phoebe's father. The punk shakes the water off himself like a shaggy dog, turns and leaves the garden without a word, dripping water and blood. The band starts up again, this time playing rock for the kids to dance.

Phoebe grabs my hand and pulls me away from her parents. "Follow me into my room. It's time for you to read," she says, beaming. Retribution must feel good. I've never had a chance to get back at my enemies physically. I was brought up in the film industry where backstabbing is the prevailing means of revenge. It's not too gratifying. A hand-to-hand combat is much more manly, more human.

"You've got a strong right hook."

"A friend showed me how to do it," she informs, handing me the screenplay and pointing to a chair. "Don't leave this room till you've finished reading it. I'll send up some coffee and sandwiches." She kisses me on the cheek but I grab her and kiss her strongly on the mouth.

"You look wonderful, Phoebe," I say out of breath.

"I knew you'd love my new nose," she laughs, and leaves me with the script.

I finish reading the screenplay in less than two hours without touching the sandwiches. I'd hoped it would be a good first draft but I didn't suspect it would be as good as it is. She needs to work on it a lot more before submitting it to a studio, but even as the screenplay reads right now, it is fresh, intelligent, touching, and imaginative. Of course, it is a love story, but with an original point of view. Amazingly mature writing for a young person without extensive experience.

But despite the joy I felt reading Phoebe's work, and despite her secret wish to please me with the transformation from a Jewish princess into a Wasp beauty, I feel ambivalent about the events.

I liked Phoebe the way she was before; she had more character, looked more like an individual. Now she looks like one of the thousands of movie stars in Hollywood trying to find a job. Also, I am still trying to overcome my experience with Cass. Though it seems that this chapter is finished in my life I must find a way to resolve it more satisfactorily.

I open the window overlooking the garden and search for Phoebe. She looks up at me as I wave the closed script. She runs across the lawn and into the house.

My arms are ready to embrace her as she enters with gleaming eyes. I don't say anything but hug her forcefully for a long moment.

"It's a wonderful work, Phoebe. I am very proud of you." I kiss her and lead her to the bed.

"Are you going to direct it?" she whispers. I don't answer. Slowly, I close my eyes, trying to decide to whom to make love.

THE END

9 780738 819907